D0174917

POSED FOR MURDER

POSED FOR MURDER

Meredith Cole

Minotaur Books ☙ New York

This is a work of fiction. All of the characters, organizations, and events portrayed in this novel are either products of the author's imagination or are used fictitiously.

A THOMAS DUNNE BOOK FOR MINOTAUR BOOKS.
An imprint of St. Martin's Publishing Group.

 Printed in the United States of America. For information, address St. Martin's Press, 175 Fifth Avenue, New York, N.Y. 10010.

www.thomasdunnebooks.com
www.minotaurbooks.com

Library of Congress Cataloging-in-Publication Data

Cole, Meredith.
Posed for murder / Meredith Cole. —1st ed.
p. cm
ISBN-13: 978-0-312-37856-1
ISBN-10: 0-312-37856-4
1. Women photographers—Fiction. 2. Photography—Exhibitions—Fiction. 3. Young women—crimes against—Fiction. 4. Murder victims—Fiction. I. Title.
PS3603.04295P67 2009
813'.6—dc22

2008034809

First Edition: February 2009

10 9 8 7 6 5 4 3 2 1

In memory of my grandmother Margery Edson-Gould, a wonderful role model whose enthusiasm for life was always contagious, and Marilyn Wallace, a great mentor, editor, and writer.

ACKNOWLEDGMENTS

Many thanks to St. Martin's Press for their sponsorship and commitment to new writers through the Best First Traditional Mystery Competition with Malice Domestic. Special thanks to Luci Hansson Zahray for pulling my work from the pile, to Ruth Cavin for helping me polish and shape it, and to Toni Plummer for all her help and endless patience. To Faith Hamlin and Courtney Miller-Callihan for all their support and assistance.

To my writing group, Triss Stein, Jane Olson, and Marilyn Wallace, for reading my book at every stage and giving comments. To Rachel Liebling, for helping to bring Lydia to life, and for always having a lot of ideas. Many thanks to all my readers, including Evelyn Edson, Mary-Frances Makichen, Vincent Casey, Chris Grabenstein, and Margaret George. I must also thank all my fellow Sisters in Crime and MWA members for their friendship and advice, and the Guppies for their enthusiasm and applause.

Thanks to the Writers Room and to the New York Foundation

for the Arts for making me feel like a professional, and to all the cafes in Williamsburg that let me sit for hours with one cup of coffee.

Thanks also to Robert Knightly and friends from the NYPD for answering my questions about police procedure. Their help was invaluable, and any mistakes are all mine.

I must also acknowledge my Springtree family for giving me a childhood full of life, laughter, and reading, and for giving me an artist's residency when I needed it most. And last, but not least, to Peter, for always making sure I have the time to write, and to Sebastian, for sometimes allowing Mommy to type.

POSED FOR MURDER

Chapter 1

She had never killed so many people in so many ways.

Lydia McKenzie stepped back and surveyed her work. Each corpse had been laid out gently and artistically, and if it weren't for their wounds or twisted limbs, they would look as if they were peacefully asleep. The light and shadows on each photograph were well defined and the contrast was crisp. Each black-and-white print was twenty by thirty inches, the largest size she had ever done, and bordered by expensive sleek black frames.

On the opening night of her show, Lydia felt like a genius. But that didn't stop her from being nervous.

"What if no one wants to buy them?" Lydia found herself expressing her deepest, darkest fear out loud. "What if no one wants a picture of a dead body on their wall?"

Georgia Rae, Lydia's best friend, considered the question. "Sugar, they can't help but be intrigued."

But Lydia could only worry. Her first New York solo show was set up at the Bulan Gallery in the ultrahip art community of Williamsburg, just across the East River from Manhattan's Lower East Side, and she was savvy enough to know she had to sell in order to get another show. For five years, she had sweated over the pictures, researching the cold cases, scouting the locations, finding the right outfits, convincing friends to lie in uncomfortable poses for hours, pretending they had been strangled, shot, or stabbed, and here was the end result of her efforts in black and white on the gallery walls. While her prints lay safe and warm in her portfolio case, she could only dream of this moment, but now she was here, exposed and open for criticism.

Her palms felt damp. She smoothed her hands over her vintage suit, wondering if she looked okay. She needed a drink.

Lydia looked around the room. There wasn't a wine bottle in sight, and Jacques Bulan, the owner of the Bulan Gallery, had vanished. "I guess Jacques hasn't set up the bar yet. . . ."

"It's still early. We'll toast your success later." A few well-dressed people wandered in and scanned the room. Their cheeks red from the cold, they looked like they had traveled all the way from Manhattan and were disappointed to be the first to arrive. Georgia, seeing an opportunity to exercise her southern debutante roots, glided across the room in her red sparkly stilettos to greet them.

Jacques, sensing potential customers, emerged from the back. He was just a little taller than Lydia, who at five seven was tall for a woman but short for a man. He had dealt with his early balding by shaving his head completely, which fooled no one. He dressed all in black and liked his clothes tailored.

"Lydia," he said, squeezing her arm, "the work looks amazing, don't you think?" With his French accent, the word *amazing* took on a brand-new zing.

Lydia tried not to cough when the fumes from his cologne hit the back of her throat. He had drenched himself in the stuff, probably to mask the scent of alcohol. Lydia had never deluded herself that Jacques loved her work. He merely hoped it was just controversial enough to make some waves in a neighborhood with galleries on every block. Competition was fierce—and he calculated that her photo re-creations of cold-case murder victims shot in a film noir style would garner lots of publicity for his gallery.

"Jacques, what happened to the drinks?"

Jacques looked around vaguely. "Drinks? I thought you were taking care of that."

Lydia's stomach dropped down into her Doc Martens and refused to come back up again. If Jacques had told her earlier, she could have figured out what to do about it in advance. But right now, she was left with two very bad choices. She could either have no wine at her opening, thereby ensuring that the droves of people arriving would turn and scurry out as quickly as they had come, or she could dip into her meager checking account and take care of it. Her credit-card balance currently hovered somewhere near astronomical.

Before she could manage to mutter anything to Jacques to show him her fury, he flitted away to greet some new arrivals. Lydia looked across the room and caught Georgia's eye. Georgia instantly recognized the pained expression on her face and came over.

"What's the matter?"

"You can hold me back before I murder Jacques Bulan with my bare hands."

"What's he done now?" Lydia was reminded yet again that Jacques had never been easy to deal with. He had insisted on expensive frames, he had made her pay the cost of printing the invitations, which was not normal, and he had been too drunk to help her hang the show. She couldn't let him ruin the biggest night of her life, the opening she had been working for ever since she arrived in New York from Dayton, Ohio, with dreams of becoming an art star and replicating the career of heroes like Cindy Sherman.

"There's no wine. We need wine!" Lydia moaned. A guy wearing flip-flops, despite the cool temperatures outside, looked over at her curiously. She ignored him. "Please take my credit card and buy some at the liquor store. And get some cups!"

Georgia nodded and marched off briskly on her mission, despite her completely impractical shoes. Lydia reminded herself that Georgia would probably use her southern charm to enlist a cute single guy to help her lug everything back, and tried to relax and enjoy her party. She had not quite reached the limit on her credit card, and she would be getting her day-job check next week.

Leo and Frankie D'Angelo, her bosses, came in carrying tall stacks of pizza boxes. They were private detectives, and she was their girl Friday. She had imagined that once she started working for them, she would get to go on stakeouts and take surveillance photos. Instead, her job was to deal with dull paperwork and answer the phone. She was starting to get restless.

Lydia moved toward Frankie and Leo, pleased that they had made the effort to come. She wasn't sure how she should greet the D'Angelo brothers. She didn't kiss them on the cheek when she came into the office every day, and she hoped the boxes in their arms would make any bodily contact impossible.

The D'Angelos looked completely out of their element in the Williamsburg art scene. They had grown up in the Italian section on the other side of the Brooklyn-Queens Expressway, where Thursday nights meant gathering for dinner at their mama's restaurant.

Mama herself appeared in the doorway behind them, dressed in a fuchsia pantsuit with sequins on the lapel. Her dyed black hair was teased into a beehive, and her eyes danced with excitement.

"Lydia!" Mama D'Angelo boomed, grabbing Lydia in a big Chanel No. 5 and garlic hug. "You look gorgeous! I hope you don't mind—I brought a few snacks for your show. Cannoli, focaccia, bread sticks . . ." Mama was a fantastic cook and her Italian restaurant was always packed. Old-timers and hipsters alike embraced her simple but delicious cooking.

"Thanks so much. That was so thoughtful of you." Lydia was touched. And more than that, she was hungry. She peeked in one of the boxes and swiped a cannoli.

"Congratulations," Leo said gravely, looking anywhere but the walls. She'd overheard him telling Frankie that he found her work morbid, but he was too polite to say anything to her face. Leo was tall and thin and always serious. His brother, Frankie, was shorter, chubby, and far more easygoing. They shared the same curly brown hair, and always dressed identically in oxford-cloth shirts, khakis, and loafers. Lydia suspected Mama D'Angelo still picked out their clothes, intent on keeping them boys forever.

"Where should we put the food?" Frankie asked. Lydia noticed for the first time that he was wearing a tie that had snowmen on it. He normally didn't dress up like that, and she wondered if it was in honor of her show. She located Jacques and turned the treats over to him. He didn't look thrilled to deal with the food, but she didn't care. He could do a little work for a change.

A few hipster types wandered into the gallery and spent a few moments looking at the work before they took off for the next event. They seemed to be searching more for the coolest party than the coolest art. But before Lydia could sink into despair, Georgia strolled in carrying a stack of paper cups, while two handsome guys staggered under the weight of the wine. Jacques magically appeared and began to set up the bar.

"You're a lifesaver," Lydia muttered to Georgia under her breath as they watched Jacques skillfully wield his corkscrew.

Georgia just smiled. She was not only a hairdresser, responsible for all Lydia's color changes and radical new looks, but she was also her best friend. "Did you think some more about the class I told you about?"

Lydia was embarrassed to admit that she had thought of nothing but her show for the past couple of weeks. "Which one?"

"I told you that my theater group signed up for a totally cool self-defense course for women, and I think you should take it, too." After a disturbing experience with a stalker fan, Georgia had recently made the transition from punk-rock lead singer to musical-theater star in a homegrown production about violence against women.

Lydia grimaced. Georgia had talked her into going to an acting class once, and she had found the experience excruciatingly uncomfortable. She hated classes that were supposed to help you get in touch with your inner self. In yoga classes, she always ended up sitting and gritting her teeth, unable to think of anything but the seconds ticking by. She imagined a self-defense class for actors would require them to pretend they were as strong as trees in the face of danger, or some similar nonsense.

"You need to learn to defend yourself if you're ever going to go on stakeouts for those detectives," Georgia said.

"You already signed me up for it, didn't you?" Lydia said, guessing, and knew she was right when Georgia pretended to study her bloodred fingernails. She knew that Georgia Rae would nag her endlessly until she said yes, so she reluctantly decided to give the class a try.

She was pleased to see that a lot of the eccentrics had arrived, making the event a typical gallery night. An elderly woman in a moldy fur coat ate four slices of pizza in rapid succession and had tomato sauce all around her mouth. A man who looked homeless, but who, Lydia knew, was a professor at the Pratt Institute, wandered around aimlessly. A group of wanna-be models slurped wine, carefully positioned with their backs to the artwork and their attractive fronts to the door. And guys with huge sideburns and nerdy dark glasses stood around holding their skateboards, trying to attract the attention of the girls by ignoring them.

A few friends from her art-critique group were milling around by the food, trying to look happy for her and not too jealous. They were fellow photographers and painters who visited one another's studios and gave feedback on the work they saw. Lydia had been in their shoes more times than she could remember, so she knew exactly how they felt: lousy. Tonight, she reminded herself, is my night. She sipped wine, accepted compliments, and tried not to look to see whether or not any red stickers had appeared, signifying that someone had bought one of her prints. Not everyone buys on opening night, Lydia reassured herself. Her show would be up for a month, and she hoped the sales would happen later on.

Lydia turned toward the door just in time to see a handsome Latino guy in his thirties walk in. He was wearing a trench coat and looked like he had been searching for one of Williamsburg's better-known restaurants but had made a wrong turn. He had on plain black shoes, which told her nothing. If the shoes had been an ice-cream flavor, they would have been dull old vanilla. But the woman who followed him in, whose blend of African and Asian features made her look like Tiger Woods, had on brown suede boots that were more like mocha fudge swirl.

Lydia went over to where her darkroom buddies and Georgia were hanging out. She wanted to hear them tell her again how great the show was going, and how good she looked in her colorful 1940s tweed suit. She loved the way old clothes were always made with so much more care, and it was usually a pleasure to wear them. She had paired the suit with a cream silk blouse with a plunging neckline, and then had pulled on a pair of black Doc Martens. The clunky boots, she reasoned, helped keep the outfit from becoming a strictly authentic costume. All the while, she kept an eye on the odd couple as they walked over to the wall and began to study her work.

"That guy seems to really like that piece," Georgia whispered in Lydia's ear. "Maybe you'll get a sale tonight after all."

The couple had stopped in front of one of the photos and appeared to be transfixed. The photo was a re-creation of the death of a runaway teenager. She'd been found, strangled and dumped on a pile of trash, in an abandoned factory building in 1981. Her whole life had been in front of her until a heartless killer who preyed on the young and innocent had stolen it from her. Lydia's friend Marie had acted as the girl, and had heroically lain amid the debris for hours while Lydia struggled to get the light just right for the shot. Lydia had dressed her like a girl who had come to New York to party. She wore a gold tube top and flowered bell-bottoms. Having positioned Marie in a pool of available light from the windows, only hinting at the girl's death by strangulation, Lydia had artfully arranged a scarf around her neck. The model's back was to the camera, but one white arm was flung out on the ground, as if beseeching the viewer to do something.

Lydia wondered what, exactly, about the photograph had caught the pair's attention. The other pictures in the room were just as dramatic and just as tragic, but neither of them spared them a single glance.

The man turned away from it, his brow furrowed. Lydia's heart sped up. She had wondered if her work would ever help identify the victims of the crimes and give peace to their families. She wondered if she had somehow seen someone who knew something about the case. She began to move toward the man, but Jacques had managed to stagger over faster.

"Here's a price list. Lydia does such charming work, don't you think?"

"Is the photographer here?"

"But of course!" If Jacques thought this man was going to buy something, he was clearly too drunk to see what had caught the man's attention. Jacques smiled and beckoned to Lydia.

"Hi, I'm Lydia McKenzie," she said, and held out her hand to him. She wondered if he was missing a family member, and tried to speak as gently as she could. She found it difficult to meet his gaze, though. He had an intense stare, which felt as if he were digging into all the corners of her brain to figure out who she was. After a moment, he shook her hand.

"Detective Romero, New York Police Department." Detective Romero flashed his credentials with the grace and speed of a veteran on the force. "This is my partner, Detective Wong. We need to speak to you for a few moments about your . . . pictures. Is there anywhere we could go to talk?"

Jacques fluttered and flitted. "Talk? If this is about those open-container laws, I can tell you that I've asked everyone to keep their drinks inside. But if someone didn't listen, there isn't much I can do. . . ."

The detective waited until Jacques was done. "And you are . . ."

"Why, I'm Jacques Bulan, and this is my gallery." Jacques made a sweeping gesture that nearly knocked him off his own feet. Lydia winced.

"Then I need to talk to you, too. Does this place have a back room or something?"

"But no one here is breaking the law, Officer. If there is going to be an interrogation, I will insist that I have a lawyer present. . . ."

Lydia had had enough. Their conversation was beginning to attract the attention of the other patrons in the gallery. The sooner they dealt with the cops, the sooner the gallery opening could get back to normal.

"There's a small office back here, Detective. We can speak privately there." Lydia led Wong and Romero to a small door. Jacques followed behind them, still bristly with indignation but blessedly quiet for the time being.

Jacques's office was utilitarian, with a large wooden desk, an elegant Macintosh computer, and a bookshelf filled with art portfolios. The walls were decorated with a few pieces from the artists he represented. There weren't enough places to sit, so Lydia pulled out a stool she had used the day before to hang photographs and perched on that.

"I'm sorry if the patrons were drinking outside the gallery. If you would like, I can close the bar." It hurt Lydia to make the offer, since she had spent so much money to make sure there was alcohol in the first place.

"No, Miss McKenzie," Detective Romero said. "This is about murder."

Chapter 2

I'm sorry, but you've made a terrible mistake." Lydia attempted a laugh but was unable to squeeze out one that didn't sound like a nervous whinny. "The photographs aren't real. They're setups with models. I discovered cold cases where the victims weren't identified and the perpetrators were never found. I used descriptions to re-create the scene of their deaths, and quite a bit of artistic license. But the models aren't really dead."

Lydia shifted uncomfortably on her stool. The silk lining of her suit usually felt sexy against her skin, but now it was soggy with sweat. She had dressed with such care for her opening, but now she felt like a mess.

"They're based on real murders?" Romero had no expression on his face. He had to be a great poker player.

"Yes, I read about them in a book called *Lost Girls.* It was a compilation of cases a reporter covered for a local paper. She described the female victims and their clothing in tremendous detail. I could really see them, and I wanted to make photographs of them. I was always curious, because none of the victims had been identified."

"She described exactly how the women were positioned and killed?"

"Yes. Occasionally, she even provided diagrams of the room."

Wong and Romero shared a glance that seemed to speak volumes, but, unfortunately, in a language Lydia didn't know. She was sensitive about her work. A lot of people thought Lydia's photos were sick. Some people thought she was nuts. Only a few people understood that by capturing the death of these people, Lydia highlighted their lives again. The victims were the homeless, the prostitutes, and the drug addicts—the discarded people who got into stranger's cars, walked bad neighborhoods, slept under bridges, and huddled in cardboard boxes. Their bodies were seldom identified or claimed. Instead, they were carted off to a pauper's grave in potter's field. Their lives had been forgotten, but she was making sure that their deaths would be remembered.

Lydia played nervously with her shoulder-length hair, currently ash-blond, courtesy of Georgia Rae's hair-coloring abilities. She usually went for red, which complemented her green eyes, but she was trying to branch out. She had never considered herself to be pretty, so she always made an attempt to look striking. Right now, with her strands of hair clinging damply to her head, she was desperate to strip off her makeup and suit and take a shower.

Romero took an invitation for Lydia's show from his pocket and placed it on the table. The photo Jacques had chosen was the same one that had so interested Romero in the gallery. "Did you take this?"

Lydia struggled for patience. "Yes. That's why it is in my show."

"Is this an actual murder?"

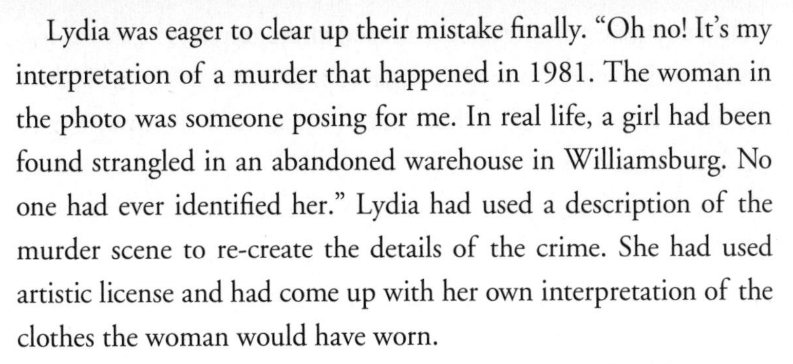

Lydia was eager to clear up their mistake finally. "Oh no! It's my interpretation of a murder that happened in 1981. The woman in the photo was someone posing for me. In real life, a girl had been found strangled in an abandoned warehouse in Williamsburg. No one had ever identified her." Lydia had used a description of the murder scene to re-create the details of the crime. She had used artistic license and had come up with her own interpretation of the clothes the woman would have worn.

Romero was probably wondering why anyone would choose murder scenes to photograph. Admittedly, it was a strange hobby for a nice girl from Dayton, Ohio. Her family was mind-numbingly normal and there was no child abuse or violence anyone could point to that might have driven her to the dark side. But one incident when she was a child had affected her more than she liked to admit. A girl named Rachel in her sixth-grade class had been kidnapped. The family had put up posters, gotten her picture on milk cartons, and people had looked for her everywhere. Lydia had not been close friends with her, but she had wondered for a long time what had happened to Rachel. She had become afraid of the dark for years afterward, and insisted that her parents come pick her up, instead of letting her walk home by herself.

Eventually, she forgot about Rachel. She began to take photographs and went to New York to college. But in the middle of her freshman year, Lydia's mother called to tell her that some hunters had stumbled across the remains of Rachel's body. Lydia had been both appalled and fascinated. She pored over the details in the paper. When she went home, she visited the site and took photographs. But there were no answers to what had happened. The police never found the killer, but Rachel's family was relieved just knowing about her death.

Lydia had done some research on the Internet and found various groups that tried to link missing persons' reports with forensic re-creations of bodies, but with little result. The sculpted aging of missing people was too static for Lydia.

Soon after, Lydia had stumbled on *Lost Girls* in a used-book store. Fascinated by the details of deaths that had happened in Williamsburg, she started trying to bring the victims to life in an effort to find out who they were.

Romero broke into her reverie. "When did you take the photograph?" She felt he had been listening to her thoughts.

Lydia wrinkled her nose. She was bad at dates. She seemed to have been working on this series forever. "Exactly?"

"Yes. As exact as you can tell us."

"It was summertime, because Marie—the model—complained about the heat and the smell of the trash in the warehouse I used. Not last summer, because I was traveling a lot then, so it must have been the summer before. I think it was in July, after the Fourth, because we found unexploded firecrackers on the floor. It was a real dump, and perfect for the photograph."

"This photo is a year and a half old?" Romero leaned back in his chair. He looked like he didn't believe a word she said.

"Approximately, yes." Lydia crossed her arms. She supposed she had proof to back up her claim somewhere, but she couldn't think of where at the moment. "Maybe if you tell me what's going on, I could help you."

Romero ignored her. "What was the full name of your model?"

"Marie LaFarge. She's a photographer, as well." Lydia noticed that both detectives became very still. The woman detective cut in with the next question.

"And who has seen it?"

"Oh God." Lydia rolled her eyes. "I don't know. I worked with Marie and one photo assistant on the shoot—I think it was my friend Georgia. And then I printed them in the darkroom I share with other photographers and hung them up to dry. Any of the others could have seen it during that process. My art-critique group saw it when they went to my darkroom several months ago. I sent out images to some galleries, but I can guarantee you that most of the owners didn't look at it."

"That's everyone?"

Lydia thought for a moment. "There's the framing shop—Union Avenue Frames, it's called—the gallerist, Jacques, and everyone who's come to the show tonight. But what does it matter?"

Romero tapped the table in front of him with a pencil. "We're not at liberty to say right now."

If the detective had been less rude, she might have held her temper and gone away meekly. But she disliked the game he was playing. "Oh, come on. I've been cooperating the best I can here. The least you can do is to tell me what's going on. You said someone was murdered."

Romero's only reaction to her outburst was to raise one eyebrow. She thought again that he must be a formidable poker player. "We're sorry for the inconvenience, but murder usually isn't a polite matter."

She was getting a very bad feeling about this. Someone had been murdered, and somehow it had to do with her photographs. And the cops thought she was involved. "Who has been murdered?"

Romero looked over at Wong. She gave a small shrug. "Marie LaFarge."

Lydia leaped out of her chair. "That's not true! I spoke to her just—" Lydia tried to remember when she had last spoken to Marie. It had probably been a couple of days ago. But Marie couldn't be dead. She was so vitally alive. She was the same age as Lydia. Lydia shook her head. "She can't be dead."

"I'm sorry. We're working on notifying her next of kin right now."

Lydia stared at Romero in shock. Nothing made any sense. The police had to have made a mistake. Maybe someone had stolen Marie's purse and been murdered. It had to be a case of mistaken identity. Marie would turn up fine and clear up the misunderstanding.

"We'd like to request that you come to the station tomorrow for questioning. And bring that book. I'd like to take a look at it."

Chapter 3

The next day, Lydia threw on black army fatigue pants, a black cashmere turtleneck sweater that had cost almost nothing because of a tiny moth hole in the sleeve, and a long black leather coat. The steel gray sky perfectly reflected her mood. She was in mourning. On her opening night, she had hoped for lots of sales, commissions, and requests for interviews. Instead, she had been told her friend Marie had been murdered, she had to report to her local precinct for questioning, and her bank account was still in danger of dipping into the negative digits.

Lydia stomped down the hall stairs of her building and felt the whole place shake. The front door didn't lock behind her, and the outside steps were encrusted with pigeon poop, but most of the time she overlooked the tenement building's flaws. Cheap rent in New York could make anyone deaf and blind. Her first order of business was coffee, and luckily the south side now had plenty of cafés to choose from. The area was divided, not always peacefully, between the

Hasidic Jews and the Puerto Ricans. To the north lived the Polish, and to the east the Italians, and more and more hipsters and trust funders were moving into anyplace they could find a spot.

The Williamsburg section of Brooklyn, the neighborhood where she lived, had originally been built for the rich in the 1800s, and then appropriated by the poor spilling out of the crowded tenements of the East Village at the turn of the last century. And then most of the neighborhood was bulldozed to make way for low-lying red- or yellow-brick factory buildings, which dominated the waterfront for years afterward. Most of the manufacturing businesses had since moved overseas, leaving a waterfront that was polluted, messy, and creepily empty. Artists looking for large spaces arrived next, converting illegal loft spaces into semilivable dwellings. Finally, rich developers swooped in to begin building luxury condominiums on every empty lot.

The D'Angelo brothers' office was in the heart of the Italian section of Williamsburg, and the entire neighborhood looked like the owners had been taken in by a particularly successful aluminum-siding salesman thirty years ago. Although the buildings were ugly, the local Sicilian community made sure the sidewalks were safe for the elderly ladies congregating on their lawn chairs into the wee hours of the night. The family who lived next door to the office had decorated their stoop with cement cherubs, covered their side yard with AstroTurf, and hung up glittery fringe in the colors of the Italian flag on their fence. On the holidays, they lighted up the block like a football stadium.

The office, on the first floor of a three-family house covered with tacky fake-stone siding, had two grimy windows and a small sign that read D'ANGELO INVESTIGATIONS: NO CASE TOO SMALL OR TOO LARGE in old-fashioned script. The sign and most of the decor had been in place since the 1950s, when the business belonged to D'Angelo senior. The brothers were either nostalgic or too lazy to update their workplace.

Lydia had been appalled by how hideous the office looked when she started working there several months ago. She had rearranged the furniture and dealt with the huge filing backup piled on every available surface. She had hung her artwork on the walls, over Leo's protests, and thrown out the dead poinsettia in the window. But until the brothers were willing to invest in a carpet to replace the present threadbare gray one, or to buy desks that weren't dented or stained, there wasn't much more she could do to spruce the place up.

Whenever she had free time, Lydia went through some of the older file cabinets and read about cases the brothers had worked on years ago. She found the details both fascinating and depressing. Parents fought over custody, insurance companies tried to catch cheaters, wives wanted pictures of the "other woman" for divorce cases, landlords wanted deadbeat tenants thrown out, and companies wanted background on future employees. Every case was a problem that the D'Angelos tried to tie in a neat bow to satisfy their clients' demands for truth and justice.

Reading through old case files, Lydia had also concluded that the D'Angelos used to be a lot busier. Most days, she answered the phone roughly eight times, not counting calls from Leo and Frankie checking in. They billed a few corporate clients regularly to be "on call," and Lydia guessed the clients' business was also a little slow. But she was amazed to find the D'Angelos' Yellow Pages entry was just a line stating the name of the company and a phone number. Most companies had to work hard to get customers, but the D'Angelos seemed content to be slow, letting their potential clients go to more aggressive private detectives.

Frankie D'Angelo was reading the newspaper with his feet up on his desk when she strode in. Luckily, he had left the gallery the previous night before the police arrived. Lydia was glad not to have to deal with his questions. She immediately poured herself a second cup of coffee from the overworked coffeemaker on the credenza. She prayed the brew was as strong as it looked.

"I hope you took a car home last night. Williamsburg is getting dangerous again," Frankie warned her from behind his paper. Gangs had run rampant in the 1970s and 1980s, but now the main crime on the street was theft. Frankie normally had a cheerful disposition, but he liked to issue warnings about everything from bad weather systems to dire political situations. He snorted and chuckled and read stories aloud from the paper, while his brother, Leo, became silent and gloomy going over the news.

Frankie waited hopefully for Lydia to take the bait. Lydia knew her duty and did not disappoint him. "What happened?"

"A girl was murdered in the industrial area. She was a photographer, too." Frankie set the paper down and watched her over his mug as he took a swig of his coffee.

Lydia's heart sank. She had called Marie's cell phone the night before, wanting to tell her that the police had somehow mixed her up with someone else and thought she was dead. When she had reached her voice mail, she had told Marie to call her. She had known something was wrong, but she couldn't wrap her mind around the idea that Marie was actually dead. Grandparents died, not vibrant women in their twenties. "Can I see?"

Frankie handed the front section of the paper over and Lydia read the headline. Marie LaFarge was dead. Everything the detectives said was true. "Oh my God," she wailed.

Frankie choked on a swallow of coffee, appalled. "You knew the girl?"

"She was my friend." Lydia stumbled over to a chair and read the details in the paper. Marie had been killed two days ago, and a homeless woman had found her body the night before on Johnson Avenue. Detectives Romero and Wong must have come from the scene of Marie's murder to the gallery when they found an invitation to Lydia's show in Marie's bag. Seeing Marie's body in a photograph on the invitation must have been a shock to the detectives.

Marie had been an amazing person and an incredible friend. She'd loved people and had always created a festive atmosphere wherever she went. She'd adored introducing friends to one another and had invented situations where creativity and conversation would thrive.

Lydia wondered if Marie had been a victim of random violence. The city was still dangerous, and there were more guns on the streets than was good for the inhabitants. Marie's death was such a senseless tragedy.

Had a violent boyfriend murdered Marie? Marie had been unusually closemouthed about her love life lately. Lydia had guessed she was taking a break from dating, but she could have met a bad seed and decided to reform him. But no, Lydia was certain Marie would have been too smart to stay in that kind of relationship. Who else would have wanted to kill her? Marie had had a caustic wit and a wicked sense of humor, which had often gotten her into trouble, but Lydia doubted either would have made anyone hate her enough to murder her.

Tears spilled out of her eyes and dripped onto Frankie's newspaper. Lydia fumbled for a tissue. She wanted more than anything to start the day over again and find Marie still alive. Marie had been so supportive of her photography, and had always been one of the first people she called when she had something good happen to her. She couldn't believe Marie was gone.

Frankie was still watching her warily, probably afraid that she was going to start sobbing hysterically. She blew her nose loudly into the tissue.

"Should I go over to Mama's and get us something to eat?" he asked anxiously.

"Nothing for me, thanks." Usually, Lydia never turned down an opportunity to eat, so she could understand why Frankie would look even more alarmed at her answer. He left the office quickly to run over to his mother's restaurant. He wasn't brave enough to stay and deal with any female tears. As soon as he left, Lydia called Georgia. She needed to talk to someone who understood how she felt.

"Did you see the paper?"

"I just can't believe Marie is dead!" Georgia's voice cracked.

"Me, neither." Lydia grabbed for a new tissue as new tears began to fall. She was grateful to have Georgia as her friend. She wondered if Georgia felt bad that she and Marie had not gotten along very well in the past six months. Lydia was still unclear what the original fight had been about, exactly. She'd tried to stay above the fray, since she loved both her friends very much, and life was too short to hold grudges.

Georgia blew her nose right next to the receiver. Lydia winced and held the phone away from her ear. "Do you think she was just randomly attacked on the street?"

"I don't know. I don't know anything about it."

"I hope this doesn't become one of those unsolved crimes. I'd hate for Marie to be forgotten like that."

Lydia thought sadly about all the cold cases she had read about in the book *Lost Girls.* Some cases languished because of overworked police departments, but sometimes the detectives involved were too lazy to follow up on leads. Detective Romero didn't strike her as lazy, but she imagined that he had more on his plate than Marie's murder.

Lydia cleared her throat. "Are you going to rehearsal later?"

"At six o'clock. I hope I can do the show without crying, though. I mean, it's all about violence against women. We want the show to help make a difference, but it's too late for Marie."

Lydia hoped that keeping busy was the best thing to do. She had her art-critique group that night. Marie had been the founder and organizer of the group, and her absence would leave a gaping hole.

"Have they finished casting all the roles yet?"

"Finally. I play an abused child and a cop, but not in the same scene. And I've got a great solo about incest."

The producers were banking on the show taking the same trajectory as hits like *The Vagina Monologues.* Perhaps a musical about domestic abuse was just what Broadway audiences were waiting for, but Lydia doubted that the people who attended were the ones who needed to be convinced that all women deserved to live without violence. Still, she was trying to be supportive of Georgia's theatrical ambitions while they lasted.

After hanging up with Georgia, Lydia realized she had to go through her meager in-box if she expected to keep getting a paycheck. Even though typing up the latest expense report from Leo was pretty mindless, Lydia still had trouble concentrating. She read over the report and saw that she had added in the same taxi ride three times. Neither the IRS nor their client would find that mistake amusing. She shook her head and tried to get back on track.

The D'Angelos tiptoed around Lydia all day, and without them looking over her shoulder, she was able to search on the Web for more information about Marie's murder. The police still hadn't let much slip, so there wasn't much available. She went to Marie's Web site and teared up again as she read the comments other friends had left about her. At closing time, she double-checked her e-mail to see where the art-critique group would be meeting. They were going to Pip Ensler's studio that night. This would be the first time they'd visited his space, and Lydia was curious about his work. Marie had brought him into the group six months ago, convinced he was a genius. Lydia knew he would be upset about Marie, since he had been a close friend. She was anxious to be with other people who remembered Marie vibrant and alive.

But first, she had an appointment at the police station to give whatever help she could so they could catch Marie's killer.

Lydia tried to get comfortable on the hard wooden bench at the station, but it was impossible. She fumbled for a roll of butter rum Life Savers that were hidden at the bottom of her purse. They were her addiction, and always managed to calm her down. She had never been to the 90th Precinct before, a white-brick building on Union Avenue, and she considered herself lucky to have escaped without having to report a theft or worse in the past. Lydia had never had much to do with the police before.

Waiting, she read all the public-service posters on the dirty beige walls about domestic abuse and personal safety and sucked on her Life Saver while she waited for the detectives to meet with her.

Finally, Detective Romero marched through the door, looking tired and disheveled, but still too handsome for his own good. He also looked like he was ready to kill someone, but hopefully he was just caffeine-deprived. She wondered if convincing them to allow her to come in at the end of the day, after work, had been a smart move.

"Follow me, Miss McKenzie." Romero sounded like a robot.

Lydia followed him down the hall without protest. Detective Wong fell into line behind them.

Romero opened the door of an interrogation room painted an institutional green and held the door for Lydia. After a moment's hesitation, Lydia went in. A large battered wooden table sat in the center of the room, surrounded by several extremely uncomfortable-looking metal folding chairs. Lydia obediently sat down in the chair he indicated. Romero and Wong sat down facing her. She imagined a row of detectives watching her from behind a one-way mirror.

Romero turned on a tape recorder sitting on the table. "I'm going to tape this conversation for the record. Do you understand?"

"Yes. Marie was a friend of mine. I want to help."

"I'm recording an interview with Lydia McKenzie." Romero checked his watch and gave the date and time. "I have to ask, for the record: Could you tell me where you've been for the last two days and nights and give me the name of anyone who can confirm your movements?"

Lydia found the situation surreal. Marie was a good friend. She would never have wanted to harm her.

"I have to ask, for the record," Romero repeated blandly.

"All week, I was at work during the day at D'Angelo Investigations, One thirty-nine Leonard Street. Ten until six. My bosses were in and out and can vouch for me. I went straight to the gallery to prepare for my show last night and I stayed until about one. Jacques Bulan was with me the entire time. And then I went home."

"Alone?"

"Yes. Alone." Lydia glared at him. "And the night before, I was pretty much home by myself except for running to a Thai place around the corner to get dinner. I don't see how this is going to help you find her killer, though. If some sicko grabbed her off the street, what do my movements have to do with anything?"

Romero ignored her comment. "Let's go through the list of people who've seen the picture. Maybe you can add to it."

"I'm sorry if this sounds stupid, but I don't understand why that photograph is important. Marie posed for other pictures, too."

"But when her body was found, it wasn't posed like it was in the other photographs."

"What do you mean?" Lydia felt the temperature drop twenty degrees.

Romero ran his hands through his already disheveled curly hair. "Someone killed Marie LaFarge and dressed and arranged the body just like it was in your photograph. And in the same location."

"But that's impossible! How could they have done it? They would have to know my photography. . . ." Lydia's voice trailed off. Now all their questions made sense. She felt so stupid not to have figured it out before. Someone had copied her photograph to kill Marie and made it—and her—part of the terrible crime. It was too horrible, and she felt both furious and impotent.

Lydia wondered what kind of person could have committed such a horrible act. To have access to her photograph, he was probably someone she knew. The only thing that could possibly be worse than having her friend murdered was the knowledge that another friend could be twisted and evil enough to have done it.

"Yes, they would have to know the way you set up your pictures. And so far, you are the only clue we have. Now let's go over that list of names again."

Lydia's head whirled as he read off the names. She tried to think of more names for him. She told him the names of as many of the other darkroom photographers as she could remember, and she reeled off the members of her art-critique group. She provided the names of the framing shop's clerks, and the gallerists. If this would somehow be helpful to the police, she was willing to do it.

"Did you bring that book *Lost Girls*?" Wong spoke for the first time. Lydia looked at her, surprised, and pulled it out of her bag. She passed it across the table to the detectives. Wong opened it and she and Romero looked it over together in silence.

"Do you think we can find the original cases that the woman wrote about?" Romero asked Wong after a few minutes.

"She seems to give enough detail. Dates and locations of the bodies. I'll call the Records Department."

"Do you think the original cases are important?" Lydia asked. She wondered if they suspected that Marie's killer was the same person who had strangled the girl in 1981.

"I don't know. But we've got to follow all leads," Romero said, shutting the book with a loud thump, which made Lydia jump. "We're keeping the details about your photographs quiet for now, okay? The killer is going to be harder to trip up if everyone knows all about how the two murders are linked together."

Lydia nodded. It was fine with her to keep her involvement quiet. She had begun her photo project with the best of intentions, never imagining that something like this could happen. In delving into the violent past of the neighborhood, she appeared to have reawakened a dangerous viper. The killer might just be getting started again.

Chapter 4

Emily opened the door to Pip's studio for Lydia, her eyes red from crying. Lydia walked into her arms and they stood there for a moment comforting each other. Lydia felt like the earth had shifted on its axis and years had gone by since her opening, instead of just twenty-four hours. She was very thankful to see that the rest of her friends were safe.

Emily was a Japanese-American woman in her twenties and was normally excited about almost everything; this was the first time Lydia had seen her upset. Usually, Emily bounced when she walked, and Lydia had not been surprised to discover she'd been a cheerleader in high school. Now she was a portrait photographer who got a lot of work doing author photos and taking employee portraits for corporations. When money was tight, she also did dog portraits. Not being much of a pet person herself, Lydia was amazed at how many people wanted formal portraits of their dogs, but Emily always found people willing to pay top dollar.

"Who could have done this to her?" Emily wailed against Lydia's shoulder. Her neat pageboy haircut was a beautiful shiny blue-black color, the kind that hairstylists could only dream about creating with chemicals.

"I don't know," Lydia said. She felt a wave of shame that it was her photograph the murderer had picked. She had not, she reminded herself, personally hurt Marie. Someone had snuffed out an amazing vibrant woman, and had imitated her photograph when the murder was committed. She took a deep breath and tried to find consolation in the fact that she was among friends.

"The police called and asked me all kinds of questions. Did they talk to you, too?"

"Yes, they did." Lydia broke from Emily's embrace. She knew the cops would ask everyone Marie had known about the circumstances leading up to her death, but she hoped they would keep quiet about the way she had been posed. Lydia looked around the room to see who else was there. A few of the artists from the group had gathered in the living room. A photographer named Rain sat glumly in an armchair, tugging at the stuffing that had begun to spill out of the arm. A spacey hippie type with long tangled black hair, she sold her photos on the streets of SoHo in Manhattan. A frown was her usual expression.

Next to Rain sat Stuart, a quiet guy on the surface but quite a daredevil by nature. He took adventure photos of people kayaking down huge waterfalls or climbing up rock faces in obscure, hard-to-reach places. He was good-looking, if you liked ruddy-faced blonds, but he had a tendency to blend into the background. Lydia had heard it hinted that there was some kind of tragedy in his family and that this had made him wary of relationships. Emily had had a big crush on Stuart for years. Lydia approved and thought they'd make a good couple, but Emily refused to make the first move, and Stuart still had not. So they were in a standoff, and Lydia had no patience for either of them.

"Hi, Lydia," Stuart said, so softly that he was barely audible. Lydia nodded, not trusting her own voice.

Pip appeared from the kitchen, wearing a trucker's cap, sunglasses, and an oversized mechanic's jumpsuit. A bushy black beard obscured the rest of his face. If his outfit hadn't been the current fashion in the neighborhood, Lydia would have assumed he was a fugitive in disguise. She really didn't know Pip well enough to give him a hug, and she wasn't sure what to say. Pip had always been rather cool to her, and she found him difficult to get to know. Marie had called him "misunderstood" and said it was difficult for him to make friends, since he was so much smarter than everyone else. Lydia was a little skeptical of that explanation. Luckily, Emily came over and did the talking for her.

"We're going to have a memorial service next weekend. I spoke with Marie's mom, and she was totally relieved that I'm arranging it. Pip knows the guys who own the Bank, and they suggested we have it there." A former loft, the Bank was an exotic bar with waterfalls and a reflecting pool. They showed movies in a large back room and had a weekly burlesque show near the bar. Normally, it would have been an odd choice for a funeral, but Marie had been a regular there. Lydia had spent many happy evenings there drinking with Marie and other friends. The Bank was a good fit.

Lydia felt like it was too soon to be talking about funerals. She hadn't even absorbed the fact that Marie was gone. Nothing seemed right. Perhaps a ceremony would help them all absorb the new reality, but Lydia wasn't ready to pull her head out of the sand.

"Will you read something?" Emily asked. "I know you guys were really close. . . ."

Lydia hated speaking in public, but she didn't think one could turn down a request like that. "Read what?"

Emily shrugged. "I'm sure you'll think of something." Lydia wished she could just go to the funeral and mourn Marie's death, but Emily was evidently intent on assigning all of them jobs.

"And ask Georgia if she'll sing, okay? Marie really loved her voice." Lydia nodded obediently.

Pip ambled over and handed Lydia a beer. She smiled at him gratefully. "Thanks," she said. Emily flitted back over to Stuart, probably to draft him for some other task.

"You looked like you needed it." Pip had a way of staring without smiling that made Lydia uneasy. It was as if the whole world were a strange problem he was trying to solve. She tried to cover up her nervousness by taking a swig from the bottle.

"Do you mind if I look around?"

"Sure, be my guest," Pip said, gesturing toward his studio area. Lydia strolled over, with Pip close at her heels. His loft was large and shaped like a U, with his living space on one side, his studio on the other, and some sort of walled off-area in the middle. Lydia rounded the corner from his living room to his studio and got her first view of his paintings. Her heart sank. She was going to have to work hard to come up with something positive to say.

"Wow," she managed to utter. "They're so . . . energetic." They were, in truth, muddy messes depicting some sort of orgy scene. But the action might have been amateur wrestling, for all she knew. Browns, grays, blues, and greens had been layered on top of one another, until it was hard to tell exactly what the point of the exercise was. She wondered if he was supremely untalented, or just didn't know enough to clean his brushes.

"Thanks," he said with a smile of satisfaction. "Picasso, Munch, and Freud have all been huge influences."

Lydia was sure all of the painters he'd mentioned would be appalled to hear it. "Have you shown them anywhere lately?"

Pip sneered. "The art scene in New York is only for the rich elite. They're a bunch of snots showing a bunch of crap."

"Not all of them—" she began, thinking his comment bordered on being cloddish, considering she had just had a show the night before.

"I did speak to Jacques Bulan a couple of months ago," Pip said interrupting her. "But he didn't really get my work. I need a gallerist who understands the subtleties of what I'm trying to accomplish."

Lydia could only wish him luck in his endeavor. She hadn't seen him at her show the night before, and now she understood that he was probably trying to avoid Jacques after a painful critique. Who could blame him?

She looked around. There was a closed door in the middle of the space, leading to yet another area. She imagined it was a large and amazing closet and that he was able to shovel any mess he didn't want seen into it. The rest of the loft was pretty clean, considering he was a bachelor living alone. She had definitely seen worse.

The loft was an enviable space. She let herself imagine for a moment how many clothes she could collect if she had the same amount of room. On the other hand, her space might be small, but the location was convenient. She had no interest in living far away from the subway, the city, and all the action on Bedford Avenue.

Lydia finished her beer quickly while Pip lectured her about his technique, and then she excused herself to go get another. All the other members of the critique group were still huddled in the living room. Emily had drifted over to comfort Jenny Powers, a plump painter who had a pile of used tissues in her lap. Lydia didn't know her well, although she had used her as a model for a photograph of Jane Doe number five. They had chatted during the shoot about this and that, but she couldn't recall a single thing Jenny had said. Jenny painted Georgia O'Keeffe–like flowers that old ladies loved. She was nice, but a little boring.

For the first time in her life, Lydia wished she photographed nice safe things like flowers, or even portraits of dogs, instead of re-created murder scenes. Flowers and dogs didn't inspire death and destruction, and she felt she had somehow caused Marie's death. She had come up with the concept, she had asked Marie to pose, and now Marie was dead. Until the police caught the killer and found out what his motivation was, she couldn't stop feeling guilty. She worried about the murderer targeting Emily, Georgia, Jenny, and Ruby, another model and unemployed dancer, and wondered what she could do to keep her friends safe.

Lydia's stomach rumbled with hunger, interrupting her morbid thoughts. She looked around the room hopefully for pretzels or chips, but all she saw was beer. The month before, Emily had hosted the gathering and had served crackers and cheese. Afterward, Marie, Emily, and Lydia had gone out to eat at a little Dominican place nearby. They drank way too many margaritas and had a great time. Lydia sighed. She was hungry and tired and she missed Marie. The critique group felt flat and dull without her energy.

Pip stood by a wall, brooding. He was probably just as depressed as Lydia about Marie. Stuart strode up to him and slapped him on the back. "Pip, man, I gotta go pretty soon. I gotta get up early for a shoot."

They shook hands and Lydia watched enviously as Stuart made his escape. Leaving too soon after him would be gauche. She would finish her beer in five minutes and then go home. She wanted pizza, hot chocolate, and sleep. And she didn't want to look at anything violent ever again.

Chapter 5

Lydia woke up on Saturday morning filled with a manic energy. Her apartment was a mess; she had some serious cleaning to do. She slipped on a Mexican housedress with large embroidered flowers and some hot-pink Chinese slippers. Marie's death made her feel strangely alive, as if she had so much to do before she could rest. She also couldn't help thinking, What if it had been me? What if my family came back and had to deal with all this mess?

There wasn't a lot of space for clutter in her apartment, with the living room turned into a giant walk-in closet, and the bedroom simply furnished with a bed, bookshelf, and television, but stacks of stuff managed to sneak in nonetheless. She'd been convinced for over five years that she was going to move to a nicer building at some point, so she'd never bothered to paint. The walls were a dull dirty white and the landlord had chosen all the fixtures with low cost as the highest priority. Right now, she had cobwebs in the corners of her apartment and her brain, and cleaning always seemed to clear her thoughts.

Her cell phone went off as she scrubbed the bathroom tile with an old toothbrush. She leapt out of the tub and had to look all over the counter before she found it. She had bought a phone that was way too small, and she was always losing it. She'd programmed the ring as the tweeting of birds. The birds grew louder and more insistent, until at last she found the phone under some junk mail. She frowned when she looked at the readout. The number wasn't one she recognized. She answered tentatively.

"Greetings from old Mexico!" Her father boomed into the phone.

"Hi, Dad." Lydia grinned. "Where are you guys?"

"In Mexico! Get it?"

"Yeah, I got it." Lydia's parents had surprised everyone by selling their house after retirement and buying an RV. They left Dayton, Ohio, two years ago and had been happily taking in the sights of North America ever since. They liked to send Lydia odd postcards from their travels, and occasionally they flew her out to meet them wherever they were staying. She had visited them at the Grand Canyon for Christmas, and she had been pleased at how relaxed they had looked.

"How did your show go? Did you get the flowers we sent?"

Lydia smiled faintly at the arrangement of mums on her counter, with a teddy bear stuck in the side on a swizzle stick. Jacques would have had a hernia if she had taken them to the gallery, so she had wisely left them at home. "Yes, I got them. Thank you."

"Your mother is grabbing the phone. Hold on."

"Honey!" Her mother's voice shook a little when she spoke now. She was beginning to sound old. Lydia had noticed changes in them over Christmas, and she worried that the next time she saw them they were going to be unrecognizable. "How was your gallery opening?"

"It was fine," she said lamely. The opening, of course, had been anything but fine, but she didn't want to worry them. If they knew what was happening, they would do something stupid, like come to New York or insist she fly out to be with them. She was fine. The killer was going to get caught and life would return to normal. Besides, she and her parents got along a lot better when they were thousands of miles apart.

"I hope you took lots of pictures! We're so sorry we couldn't have been there."

"Me, too," Lydia said, lying.

"Did you get the postcard we sent of the largest cacti in the world?"

"Nope I haven't gotten that one yet." Instead of tossing all the weird postcards that they sent in the trash, where they clearly belonged, Lydia was sticking them in a photo album to give to her parents when they got home. She knew they'd love to have the record of their travels.

"Well, you will. Your father is signaling to me that I have to wrap it up. We'll call you in two weeks, okay?" Lydia's dad was always terrified of running up large telephone bills and of using up the minutes on her cell phone. Lydia had explained to him a hundred times that she could talk as long as she wanted on weekends, but he never got it. And the only way she could reach them was by leaving a message with an answering service they'd set up before their trip.

"All right. Talk to you soon."

"Hugs and kisses, sweetie." And her mother was gone. As Lydia hit the button on her phone to end the call, she realized she was still holding the old toothbrush in her hand. For just a moment, she wished that she was little again and believed her parents could solve all her problems and protect her. But there was no pretending with the problem she had to face right now.

As usual, she had to tear apart her apartment and make a giant mess in order to clean it. She slid big piles of papers onto the floor in order to clean off her desk and kitchen table. Clothes that she wanted to get rid of were piled on a chair while she hunted for a shopping bag to put them in. If they were good quality and she was just tired of them, she tried to hawk them at one of the many vintage stores in the neighborhood. If they were embarrassingly awful, like the sweatshirt of all of Santa's reindeer, with real jingle bells sewn onto the sleeves, which her mother had bought her for Christmas, she dumped them at the Salvation Army.

One of the essential parts of feng shui, a Chinese practice she studied when she had the time, was that it was essential to remove the unessential from your life. Clutter in the corners of your apartment and the drawers of your desk led to a cluttered mind, which made it difficult for you to move forward. She gave her clothes and photographs a special waiver, but everything else she tried to purge ruthlessly when it was no longer useful.

By midafternoon, Lydia was at last seeing some progress on her apartment. She began to put things back onto clean shelves, and her mopped floors had begun to dry. She was glad to feel pleasantly exhausted. She hadn't realized how much pent-up energy she had. Marie's murder and the disaster that was her show had made her feel impotent and helpless. She had actually wanted to do something. Cleaning was a much-maligned art, but it was something.

Lydia knew Marie had family members in the Midwest whom she was particularly close to, and she imagined they had rushed to New York already. She needed to find a piece to read at the service, so she decided to go to Marie's apartment and see if they were there. Perhaps she could also help out with cleaning and organizing there. She needed to keep busy, or she was going to totally lose it. She tossed off her housedress and slipped into a pair of wool plaid capris and a red mohair cardigan that brought out the red in the pants. She scrounged for a pair of flats and warm socks, then put on her bright yellow wool fitted coat. She looked like a suburban teenager from the 1960s; all she needed was a headband.

The clouds were low and deep gray, and there was a damp bite to the air. A Queens-bound bus rumbled up just as she hit the sidewalk, and she hailed it. Marie lived in Greenpoint, the predominately Polish neighborhood in North Brooklyn. A mixture of residential, commercial, and industrial, it had not only been built years ago by the Poles but had new immigrants arriving there still. All the signs were in Polish, and it was a great place to buy blintzes, perogis, and rye bread. But the neighborhood, just like Williamsburg, was starting to be infiltrated by luxury loft buildings, and she wondered how long it would keep its unique flavor.

Lydia rang the bell at Marie's house, a gray row house with three apartments. The front door had a small window covered by a lace curtain. After a few minutes, the door vibrated loudly from the buzzer. She pushed the door open and walked into the dim hallway. The only illumination came from a small lamp over a painting of the Pope, and the dark wooden stairs were difficult to see.

The door to Marie's apartment was standing open. Lydia peered inside. "Hello?" she called.

An older woman in a pink tracksuit, who had the same tall and slender build as Marie, emerged from the kitchen holding a dish towel. "Are you from the funeral home?"

"Uh, no. I'm Lydia. I was a friend of Marie's. You must be her mom," Lydia said.

"Oh, Lydia, yes. I forgot Emily said you were coming over," Marie's mom said, twisting the dish towel around and around in her hands. She looked tired and strained and still in shock.

Emily would have to be a mind reader to know I was coming over, Lydia thought, but she let it pass. "I'm so sorry for your loss. Marie was very special, and we'll all miss her a lot." Lydia knew her words were inadequate, but she didn't know what else to say. She did miss Marie, and the apartment felt empty and forlorn without her presence.

Marie's mother nodded and blew her nose on the dish towel. "I wish the police had caught the monster who did this to her."

"I know. It's horrible to think about him still out there." Lydia wondered if the police had told her how Marie had been posed like she was in Lydia's photograph. She didn't think she'd be so warm if she had already made the connection

"I wish I could offer you a cup of tea." Marie's mother looked wistfully around the apartment.

"That's okay," Lydia said, knowing how bleak Marie's kitchen was on a normal day. "Emily asked me to read something of Marie's at the service, and I was hoping to find it on her shelf."

"Emily has been such a dear. It's been wonderful not to have to worry about the memorial service. At home, everyone would have asked why we weren't having an open casket. . . ."

Lydia managed a small, encouraging nod. Marie's mother stopped to sop up her tears with the towel.

"Is there anything else you need help with?"

"I've been looking all over for her address book, and I just can't find it. I know she had a lot of friends and people she did business with, and I want to invite them all to the service."

"It might be at the darkroom we all use. I could check her locker there."

Marie's mother sighed with relief. "Thank you. It's so hard for me to call people and tell them again and again that she's dead, but I know it has to be done."

The task was small, and Lydia felt she could definitely volunteer to do more. "If you want, I could make some calls, too. I probably know a lot of the people."

"Could you? That would be such a big help." Marie's mother made a small attempt to smile. Lydia remembered her original task.

"Do you happen to know where she kept her books?"

"I think I saw some in her bedroom."

"I'll start there, then, if you don't mind."

Once Marie's mother had returned to the kitchen, Lydia slipped her digital camera out of her bag. Looking through the lens of the camera was always good for helping her distance herself from a situation. It was painful to look at all of Marie's orphaned belongings. Marie was everywhere in the apartment and, sadly, nowhere.

Marie's bedroom was larger than the living room, and it was obviously where she had spent most of her time when at home. Her computer desk, her enormous bed, and the television were all in there. The computer was missing, probably taken by the cops, and someone had tried to do some straightening, but without much success. Marie had owned thousands of fashion magazines that she hadn't been able to part with. She'd used them for inspiration, she'd always said. She'd also bought lots of ridiculous haute couture dresses at huge discounts and had really worn them. Since she'd been a tall, skinny stick, she'd actually looked good in them.

On the bedside table was a stack of erotic women's fiction,

which wasn't at all suitable for a memorial service. Above the bed was an enormous painting of the figure of a woman. Although mostly gray and brown, it had hints of red and purple in its wildly frenetic brush strokes, which gave it a disturbing edginess. Lydia disliked it immensely, and she had a strange feeling she'd seen something like it recently. She went in closer to examine the signature at the bottom and read the name Pip. Lydia wondered if the woman in it was supposed to be Marie, and what, exactly, Marie had seen in it. Marie normally had had quite good taste.

Marie's mother came into the bedroom, and Lydia quickly slipped the camera into her pocket. "I was just admiring the painting."

Marie's mother frowned. "Yes. We're not exactly sure what to do with that. Did you find her books?"

Marie didn't seem to own anything suitable for a service, but Lydia couldn't intrude on her mother's grief any longer. "Yes, thanks." She patted her purse. "I'm sorry to come over at a time like this."

"It's fine," Marie's mom said sadly. "We still can't believe she's gone."

"Me, either," Lydia said. She reached over and impulsively gave Marie's mother a hug. It made both of them feel only a little bit better.

Chapter 6

Lydia decided to walk to Manhattan Avenue and ride the bus back home. Huge snowflakes began to fall, twisting and turning all the way down. She bent her head against the wind and started the long slog. She trudged a few blocks, slipping and sliding in her flats, before she realized that she had no idea what she was going to say at Marie's service, and now Marie's mother would expect it to be something profound, taken from Marie's own collection. She would have to ask Emily for advice again. Trusting herself to come up with a few words was so daunting. Marie's death felt too raw to her.

She didn't see any buses coming, so she continued to hike to the next stop on the route to keep her blood circulating. Her socks felt soggy and her feet were cold. Her cell phone went off. She fished it out with frozen fingers. It was Georgia.

"Hey," Lydia answered glumly. "Tell me you want to meet up for coffee. I need to vent."

"Did you forget about our self-defense class? It's going to start in ten minutes."

Sometimes the best course of action was to lie to the ones you loved. "I didn't forget. Not exactly. I don't have the address with me. I was paying a call on Marie's family."

The mention of the bereaved family put Georgia off her stride, just as Lydia had hoped. Because she was a good southern girl, Georgia's instincts would be to deliver a gooey coconut cake to the grief-stricken. "I didn't know they were in town."

"They're staying at Marie's apartment." There was a silence. Lydia knew Georgia was thinking about what her mother would do in those circumstances.

"So you're still in Greenpoint?"

"I'm almost at the park. Where are you?"

"In a basement church on Havemeyer, just below Metropolitan. Are you going to be able to come?" Georgia asked, a little more solicitously this time.

Lydia suddenly needed to be among people. She was tired of having only her thoughts for company. "I'll hurry."

Despite hurrying, Lydia was late for the class. She checked the address twice before going down skinny cement steps to enter the basement of a Spanish storefront church. All her hopes of sneaking into the class unnoticed were dashed when an attractive woman standing at the center of the students met her eyes. Her face was wide, with high cheekbones and skin the color of milk chocolate. She moved with the fluid grace of a dancer, and she was all muscle.

"Good afternoon. Please join us. My name is Martina."

"Hi, Martina. I'm Lydia," she mumbled, embarrassed. She shrugged off her coat and left it and her bag in the corner where everyone else had dumped their things.

"We've just started. We're practicing breathing from the diaphragm." If there was anything Lydia hated more than acting and yoga classes, it was people telling her how to breathe. Breathing exercises made her extremely self-conscious, and short of breath. It was as if she'd forgotten how to breathe without instructions. But Lydia joined the circle and obediently attempted to breathe deeply without hyperventilating as Martina filled them in on her background.

Martina told them that she had been raped as a teenager, and had decided not to live her life in fear, but to fight back. She'd gone on to earn several black belts in different martial arts, including karate. "And then I decided that it was not enough for me to know how to defend myself. I wanted to share the knowledge with other women. Because when you don't have skills, you are powerless. Because when you don't have a plan, you are helpless. But when you have skills and a plan, you become . . . powerful!

"Rapists and muggers are basically lazy. They want the easiest mark possible with the least amount of trouble. So we're going to exercise our troublemaking skills to fight back." Martina strode around the room, looking strong and dangerous. Lydia wished she looked half as powerful.

"Your first important skill involves your voice. Yelling will throw your attacker off his stride. He picked you in the first place because he thinks you're an easy target. It could also alert someone else, and he won't know if help is coming or not, so hopefully he will stop the attack."

Martina then taught them how to hit the weak places on an attacker's body. "It doesn't matter if he's two hundred and fifty pounds of muscle, he still has vulnerable eyes, throat, and knees. It doesn't take much strength to gouge out eyeballs. It doesn't take much force to break a kneecap and be able to run away. You can do it with a well-placed kick. Remember, you're fighting for your life here."

Lydia had a hard time imagining the twenty women in the room running around all over the city breaking men's kneecaps and gouging out their eyeballs. They looked as intimidated and grossed-out as she felt.

"Let's pair up and practice together."

Lydia found Georgia before her friend could pair up with some actor she knew, and grabbed her arm. "You'd better be my partner, after dragging me here."

"Isn't she amazing? She's so inspiring." Georgia made goo-goo eyes at Martina across the room. "I can't imagine going through what she did and refusing to be a victim like that."

Lydia had to admit that Martina was inspiring, but it was doubtful that any of them would have a black belt or big muscles by the end of six lessons. It wasn't exactly false advertising, but it was a little difficult to gauge what they were actually going to learn in the class.

They practiced yelling no as loudly as they could and each pretended to strike her partner's eyes with fingers, hit her throat, and kick her kneecaps. Kicking with fitted capri pants was challenging, and Lydia prayed she wouldn't rip them. One woman was accidentally kicked, and class halted for a moment to make sure she was okay. She got back up after a few minutes and smiled gamely. Luckily, a kick to the knee didn't appear to be as effective as Martina claimed. After that, they tried their new skills on a gymnastic-style blue pad laid against the wall.

"Hit him! Get him! Go, go, go!" Martina stood next to the pad and yelled encouragement to each of them, and urged them all to do the same. So as each woman went up and beat the crap out of the pad, they all yelled for her. The exercise felt ridiculous at first, but then it grew more and more exciting. When it was Lydia's turn, she felt like a champion boxer cheered on by fans. She hit the pad harder than she thought she could and felt a huge adrenaline rush.

All too soon, the class was over. They were given essays on self-defense to read and told to come back a week from Sunday. Lydia located her coat and bag and strolled outside with Georgia. She was absurdly glad that Georgia was taking the class, and she wished Ruby, Jenny, and Emily had signed up, too. Somewhere out there, a killer could be looking for his next victim, and she knew she would be happier if all of them had the skills to fight back.

"I forgot to tell you that Emily wants me to talk at Marie's memorial service at the Bank, and she'd like you to sing something."

Georgia looked pleased, as Lydia knew she would. "Really? I'd love to. What should I sing?"

"Nothing boring, not what people normally sing at those things. You know how Marie was."

"Maybe Emily will have some ideas." They were both deferring to Emily's memories of Marie, and it felt strange. It reminded her of a televised tragedy with lots of attractive blond girls claiming to be the victim's "best friend." Emily seemed strangely driven to take charge of every aspect of the service for Marie, and Lydia wondered if Emily was guilty of something. She felt odd suspecting someone so innocuous and cheerful, but people always claimed that murderers were just like normal people.

Chapter 7

Sunday morning, the menacing roar and ominous scraping of a snowplow digging out Williamsburg jolted Lydia awake. A quick peek out the window revealed a world covered in snow. There were probably just a few inches on the ground, but the whiteness of the snow covering the trash on the street made even the chain-link fence across the street look mysterious and magical. The snow gave Lydia the perfect excuse for staying home. But she remembered her promise to Marie's mother. She needed to look for Marie's address book at the darkroom and call everyone to tell them about the memorial service the following weekend. She hoped the killer hadn't found Marie's address book, because then there would be no hope of getting it back. She supposed she could ask the police detective, but she doubted he would want to cooperate with her.

She put on fuchsia long johns and a long gray wool skirt with a provocative six-inch slit up one side. She dug up a hot-pink cashmere sweater that was toasty. Then she slipped on a pair of furry boots that looked like they could have been used by a member of a Victorian Arctic expedition, but they were far preferable to the flats she'd worn the day before. Once she put on her coat, she felt like the abominable snowman, but she knew she was going to be warm.

Lydia walked down the street, passing an evangelical storefront church that was literally rocking out. The Baptist movement had taken hold in a big way in the Latino community, and storefronts had been converted to small evangelical churches. They were quiet during the week, but on Sundays electric guitar music and amplified voices spilled out of the open doors, and women dressed in high heels and skirts, men dressed in black pants and white shirts, and little girls dressed in frilly dresses all spilled out onto the sidewalk. The singing and clapping intrigued Lydia as she strolled past on her way to the darkroom: it was quite different from the dry Methodist services she'd sat through in Dayton. She imagined that a similar scene was unfolding in the basement where her self-defense lessons were held.

Lydia paid membership dues to belong to a darkroom studio in the industrial park in East Williamsburg. The members ran it cooperatively, and they kept their fees low by renting out a photo-studio space when the members weren't using it. Some clients skipped the studio and went straight to the building's roof for the ultimate grimy urban feel. The building was sandwiched between abandoned factories and a housing project on the edge of Bedford-Stuyvesant, and the view from the roof reeked of urban decay. There were lots filled with abandoned cars, boarded-up buildings, and fences covered with graffiti. The location was great for a studio because there was nothing to do there but work.

As she opened the front door of the studio space, she was greeted by the strong smell of chemicals. She inhaled happily, wishing she had some prints she could work on. Printing could be addictive, and she'd lost many hours in the darkness trying to make her prints perfect, burning in the sections that needed more shadows and covering other parts from the enlarger's strong light to keep them from getting too dark.

The place appeared to be deserted. Since they had a commercial lease, the heat was turned off on the weekends, and very few members braved potential frostbite. Just as she was beginning to believe she was all alone, Rain, wearing a tie-dyed caftan, dashed out of the small bathroom near the front door. She shrieked when she saw Lydia.

"You scared me to death!" Rain exclaimed. "Where did you come from?"

Lydia had to stop herself from rolling her eyes. Leave it to Rain to try to make her feel guilty about coming into her own darkroom to work. Rain's express purpose in life appeared to be to make everyone feel guilty about something: that they weren't doing enough to end world hunger, that they weren't protesting against the killing of endangered species, or that they weren't single-handedly feeding all the homeless.

Lydia took a breath so she wouldn't say something sarcastic. "Sorry. I guess we're all on edge right now." Lydia didn't care much for Rain or her photographs. She had always assumed Rain sold sentimental photos of the World Trade Center on the streets of SoHo because she couldn't find a gallery for her work.

"Isn't it terrible about Marie? I can't believe anyone could have killed her. It must have been one of those crazy sexual deviants who pick their victims at random. Or a serial killer." Rain was addicted to *CSI* and a host of other cop shows on TV, although she always swore that she hadn't trusted the police since her run-ins with the law during her student protest days. Lydia made a point of not taking anything Rain said seriously.

"Did you hear anything about how she was . . . um . . . posed?" Lydia asked. She wanted to know if the police had been asking people about her photographs yet.

"Posed?" Rain shuddered. "I didn't hear anything about that. Don't crazy perverts and religious zealots usually do that kind of thing?"

Lydia didn't know. But she assumed that all murderers, unless they had struck out in a moment of passionate anger or desperation, were crazy. Taking a human life was not something that sane people usually saw as the solution to their problems. Although she had dealt with death with her photographs, she believed she was making a statement about violence against women. She didn't feel that she had anything in common with a killer who stamped out human life.

Rain leaned in theatrically, as if she was afraid of being overheard. "I heard that the cops came by yesterday and asked everyone questions. They were particularly interested in Emily and Stuart."

Lydia felt a familiar twinge of annoyance at Rain. She was sure the police were questioning everyone whom Marie had known, not just Emily and Stuart. Rain just liked to feel she had an inside track.

Rain's cell phone rang to the tune of a Doors song. She examined the readout window. "It's one of my collectors calling. I have to take this."

Lydia watched her bustle away to talk to her "collector." She told herself that she didn't feel a single pang of jealousy about Rain earning a living from her art while she herself worked in an office to make ends meet. Mostly, Lydia was glad not to have to take the sentimental photographs of puppies, kittens, and New York landmarks that Rain did to cater to the tourist trade. She preferred more challenging stuff. And if no one was going to pay her for the challenging stuff, then she would gladly pay her rent by working for the D'Angelos.

Lydia walked over to the row of industrial-strength gray lockers the members had picked up for the studio at a factory-closing sale. She used a green padlock with a key for her locker because she was terrible at remembering random numbers. Inside were neat stacks of paper for printing, depleted somewhat after her printing frenzy before the show. On the shelf were rolls of film, filters for printing, an extra lens, a bag of butter rum Life Savers, a half-empty bag of pretzels for emergencies, and her portfolio.

Printing only a limited edition made each of her photographs more valuable, so she had made only ten copies of each of the photographs hanging in her show. Lydia framed one copy, at enormous cost to herself, and the other nine she stored in the portfolio case. She took out the portfolio and paged through the photographs until she came to the set based on the murder. She shuddered when she saw the print, imagining Marie's pain and suffering for the first time. She had not considered it when creating the photograph, but now the girl's death and Marie's felt too real. She hoped their deaths had been quick, for their sakes.

With a deep breath, she forced herself to concentrate again on the problem at hand. She tried to ignore the image in the photograph as she counted the prints. There were only eight. I must have made a mistake, she thought. She had made ten, fitted nine into the plastic sleeves herself, and framed the tenth for her show. Lydia started over and counted them again. She got the same result. Her mind whirled and her hands went clammy.

All nine should have been there. She was positive that she had put them all into the portfolio. She scanned the inside of her locker to make sure she had not misplaced one of them. Her heart seized as she realized that the print probably had been stolen. Someone had taken the photograph and then used it as a blueprint for Marie's murder.

It still didn't make sense that someone would have wanted to kill Marie. And it made even less sense that the killer would have used Lydia's photograph to do so. The missing print pointed to her theory that the killer was someone she knew. Possibly Marie had known the murderer, too. But she didn't understand why that person would have posed Marie as she appeared in Lydia's photograph unless he wanted to make Lydia look guilty. She was terrified of the murderer's true intentions, but angry that he would kill one of her friends.

Lydia's eyes moved down the row of lockers until they came to number 72—Marie's locker. Marie had given Lydia the combination once so she could take out a package for a courier who was stopping by while Marie was on a shoot in Los Angeles. She'd bought a programmable lock, and she'd used her birthday as the combination: 02-14. Marie had thrown a big Valentine-themed birthday party for herself every year, so Lydia could remember her birthday with no difficulty. She wanted to open the locker and see if she could find Marie's address book. She might be able to piece together some kind of idea of who might have killed Marie.

Lydia moved quickly down the row to Marie's locker. She felt like she was doing something illicit, even though Marie's mom had given her permission to search it. She quickly dialed the combination. The lock didn't budge. She was afraid Marie might have changed the combination before she died, but when she dialed in the combination again, going a little more slowly this time, and pulled hard, the cranky old lock snapped open with a creak that sounded almost like a sigh. She slid the lock out and opened the locker door.

The inside of the door was decorated with images from Marie's recent trip to India. She had fallen in love with the country, and taken some of the best photographs of her career there. She had scored a show downtown and printed the images as three-foot sepia squares on white cotton cloth. The photographs were mostly of women and children, and the sepia on the cloth somehow made them look timeless. Lydia's favorite was of a group of children bathing in a river. The air from the gallery's heating vents had buffeted the material, making the children look like they were dancing.

Lydia had been envious of Marie's exciting adventures at the time, but now she was happy that her friend had had the experience and such a successful show before she died. Lydia still had time left (she hoped) to travel the world and have more shows of her own.

Marie had always been generous with her things and with herself, but she had never been neat. The locker was a jumbled mess. Lydia carefully paged through a stack of miscellaneous papers and prints. In the pile were old negatives, snapshots from Marie's last birthday party, and a pocket-size weekly planner and address book filled with notes. Lydia was glad to find the address book. She did not have time to study the photographs, but she thought that perhaps Emily could use them somehow at the service. Lydia put the photographs and the planner into her bag to study later.

She lifted out a pile of Marie's fashion prints and looked through them. They were recent photos of up-and-coming designers' strange, unwearable clothing, and unlike the lighting in Marie's other photos, the lighting in these made them look oddly flat. She wondered what had been happening with Marie's fashion-photography career. She'd heard it was taking off, but the photographs looked uninspired. There was none of the joy that Lydia found in the photos of India.

Lydia was almost at the end of the stack when her missing print fell out onto the floor at her feet. She stared at it in horror. Had Marie taken her photograph? That didn't make any sense at all. But if she hadn't, then what was it doing in her locker? If someone else had taken it and placed it there, that person had to know the combination of Marie's locker, too.

"What are you doing?" Lydia whirled around, to see Detectives Romero and Wong standing a few feet behind her. They did not look happy to see her.

Chapter 8

"One of my prints was missing," Lydia stammered. "I just found it in Marie LaFarge's locker."

Detective Romero took out a large white handkerchief from his coat pocket. Men rarely carried real cotton handkerchiefs these days, but she guessed he had an old-fashioned streak. He bent down to pick up the print at her feet, using his handkerchief to protect it from fingerprints. He held it up to Wong, who leaned forward and studied it.

"Miss McKenzie, how many people besides you know the combination to the victim's locker?" Wong asked. Lydia had a hunch that Wong didn't like her much. Some women were like that. They got bristly and territorial when anyone with estrogen was in their vicinity. She decided the best policy was just to be polite. After all, when dealing with the police, polite was always a good thing.

"I don't know. Marie wouldn't have thought twice about giving it out if she needed someone to grab something for her from her locker or if someone needed to borrow something. That was just the way she was." Marie was unusually trusting. Perhaps that was her downfall, but that was also what had made her a wonderful person.

"How long have you known the combination?" Romero asked.

"Six months?" replied Lydia, guessing. "Her mother asked me yesterday to look in her locker." She didn't intend to tell them why. If she brought up Marie's address book, they would probably demand that she hand it over.

"You should have contacted us first. You may have ruined valuable evidence by going through her locker," Romero said. There was no way that she wanted to inhibit their inquiries, but she wondered if they would have even thought to look in Marie's locker on their own. Lydia felt a little guilty about hiding the planner and the snapshots from them, but she seriously disliked their attitude. She made a promise to herself that she would give the things up as soon as she had a chance to go through them and call Marie's clients about the funeral.

"Detectives," Lydia said, biting her lip. "I have cooperated in every way that I could with your investigation. I just want my friend's killer caught."

Wong and Romero exchanged a glance. "Would you object to us looking in your locker?" Wong asked. Lydia did. Greasy fingerprints and too much handling ruined photographs, but she imagined that it would not be to her advantage to disagree. She stepped aside and gestured to her locker.

"It's the one with the green lock," she said. "It's open."

To Lydia's relief, Wong slipped on a pair of gloves before she went over to Lydia's locker. Romero also pulled on a pair, but his focus was Marie's locker. He began systematically to go through the contents while Lydia stood by and tried to pretend she wasn't watching either of them. She tried not to wince as Wong touched everything or pulled out embarrassing items like tampons or notes from ex-boyfriends. She made a mental note to clean her locker thoroughly before becoming involved in a police investigation again.

Romero filled up a plastic bag with the contents of Marie's locker, then fastened the lock on the door. The lock shut with a snap that seemed to echo through the space. He moved over to join Wong at Lydia's locker.

Wong, having finished examining the contents of Lydia's locker, was scrutinizing the door. "Does anyone else have a key?"

Lydia shook her head. "Nope. I have the only one on my key ring."

"And when did these scratches appear? Could someone have broken in recently?"

"Those scratches predate me, I think. The lockers have always been beat-up, and I doubt I would have noticed if someone had broken in." Now that Wong mentioned it, the locker did look like it had acquired a few fresh scratches.

"But you noticed a print was missing."

"Yes, but that's because I have only a limited number of them."

"Why? You could make as many as you want, right?"

"Yes, but that would make them diminish in value."

Wong looked at her blankly. She and Romero very likely knew nothing about art. "I have to tell people when they buy my work how many copies I'm making, so they know that they're getting something rare. If I made thousands of copies, it would be like owning a poster or something, so I mark each print one of ten, two of ten, et cetera."

Romero, who had been listening in, now entered the conversation. "When did you notice it was gone?"

"Today. So it could have been taken anytime after I printed them two weeks ago. I remember them all being there when I put them in my portfolio, so I guess it couldn't have been taken while the prints were drying." Lydia was very methodical about her portfolio, so the second scenario was extremely unlikely.

"How many members belong to the darkroom studio?"

"About thirty, I think. I have a membership directory somewhere."

Romero nodded. "I have one of those, but it doesn't tell me how many photographers came in regularly."

Lydia wrinkled her nose. "I guess about twenty. Some come only in the middle of the night and some only during the day. There's always equipment available, though."

"Do guests ever come here?"

"Occasionally, someone will bring a friend in for company, or a client to see his or her work. Or an outsider will rent our studio. But it's rare. Mostly, we just come here to get work done."

"Show me where you hang up your prints." He made it sound like an order, not a request, and Lydia didn't care for his tone. As she walked toward the darkroom, she reminded herself that she was doing this for Marie. Romero followed close behind her, with Wong trailing along.

The entrance to the darkroom was a circular revolving door, not unlike the glass doors designed to keep climate-controlled air inside stores and office buildings. But this door was made of solid wood and painted black. Its purpose was to keep light from reaching the darkroom. Lydia stepped inside and pushed the door around until she came out on the other side into the darkness. It took a moment for her eyes to adjust to the lack of light, but strategically placed red safelights kept the room from becoming pitch-black. The door spun around again and Romero emerged behind her. Another spin ejected Wong into the darkness.

"Hey—where are the lights?" Wong said, annoyed. Lydia smiled. Wong had probably gone straight from dropping film off at the drugstore to buying a low-maintenance digital camera. If she knew nothing about printing photographs, she would need the most basic tour.

"This room is kept dark at all times so the paper we use for printing and the film aren't accidentally exposed to the light. The machines are called enlargers." There were eight enlargers of varying quality on counters at waist height, and underneath them large jugs of chemicals were stored. In the center of the counter was a giant rectangular sink, and inside were the trays of developer and fixer and the rinse baths. Over the sink hung clotheslines with clothespins attached, where a few drying prints and negatives dangled.

"How does it work?"

Romero sounded truly curious, so Lydia took a deep breath and explained. "You put the negative in the enlarger and when light shines through, it creates the reverse image, or how we see with our eyes. Light areas become dark and dark areas become light. Once I choose the length and the strength of the light, it exposes special paper with the image. Then I put the paper in the developer to bring out the image, the stop bath to stop the process, and the fixer to make the image permanent. And then it has to go into the rinse bath."

She stepped over to the center of the room, where a clothesline was strung. "This is where we hang the prints to dry."

"How long does it take them to dry?"

"Depends on the humidity. Usually about a day."

"So you just leave them here?"

"Nothing has ever been stolen. It was never a problem." We used to trust one another, she thought, before Marie was killed.

"Is anyone else here today?"

"Rain was around earlier. She was at the opening."

Romero checked his watch. "Let's see if we can find her."

They exited through the circular door and Lydia nearly collided with Rain. Predictably, Rain shrieked again. Romero stepped forward, on alert. The door spun and Wong came out with one hand on her gun.

At the appearance of a handsome man, Rain batted her eyes in a ridiculous attempt at flirtation. "I'm so sorry, Officer. I thought you were the murderer."

"Do you remember Detectives Romero and Wong?"

Rain nodded at Romero, ignoring Wong. Romero took out a pad from his pocket. "I know we spoke already, but I was wondering if you've seen anyone here lately who was new or out of the ordinary."

"Not really. Marie brought in a friend once about a week ago, and a client one day, too, I think. But that's about it. It's a slow time of year."

"Marie brought people in? Did you catch their names?"

"The client was an editor from *Beauty.* Jeanne Goldberg was her name, I believe. But I don't follow fashion much," Rain said, practically simpering. "And the friend was Pip, from our art-critique group. I think he was some sort of boyfriend, but I doubt it was as formal as all that."

"Thanks very much," Romero told her. "We'll let you know if we have any other questions."

As Rain floated away, convinced she'd made a conquest, Romero checked his notes. "I don't have information on either of them."

"Pip Ensler is a painter. He and Marie were just friends, as far as I know."

Romero put his notebook back in his pocket. Lydia noticed with annoyance that he never took notes when she gave him information. Since Lydia doubted it was because he memorized her every word, it probably meant that he didn't think it was worth noting.

"You used that book *Lost Girls* to find the cases you wanted to photograph. How did you choose which ones?"

Lydia had to think hard. "I think they were in the order that they appeared in the book. The first one was the one I did with Marie. The story appealed to me, and I really saw the visual possibilities."

Romero nodded, as if the information was exactly what he expected.

"Is that all?" Lydia asked.

"We're going to need to take a few things from your locker until we wrap up the investigation," Wong told her flatly. "Do we have your permission to do so?"

Lydia opened her mouth to ask when that would be, then shut it again. She meekly nodded her head yes. The removal of all her negatives and photographic paper would prevent her from doing any work. But she wasn't sure when she would want to work again. If her work had caused or precipitated such ugly violence, she didn't know when she would feel comfortable working on the project again. Perhaps never.

"Thank you for your cooperation," Romero said, and his cell phone went off. He pulled it out of his pocket. "Romero."

Lydia watched as his face became grim. Her heart sank. It must be hard to have a phone whose ring signals death so often, she thought. He responded in monosyllables and hung up.

"Was it about Marie?" Lydia couldn't stop herself from asking.

Romero shook his head. " A new case," he said bleakly. "It never ends."

Wong's cell phone went off next and she turned away to answer it. She already knew a new case was coming their way.

"Are you going to be okay getting home?"

"Sure," Lydia said, oddly touched that he would worry about her safety.

And with a quick wave from Romero, they were gone.

Chapter 9

Every time Lydia rooted around inside her bag at the office the next day, her hand ran into Marie's photographs and weekly planner at the bottom. Lydia felt guilty. She justified her possession of the items by reminding herself of the task she'd been given by Marie's mother. The reason she did not tackle the calls first thing in the morning and then promptly hand the planner and address book over to the police was that she had to work. The D'Angelos were not going to allow her to play hooky again. Even though business was slow, they were convinced that anyone who called the office and didn't reach a live human being automatically became a former client.

"Could you straighten up a bit? We've got a new client coming in at eleven." Frankie's idea of straightening was to pile all the coffee cups in the sink and dump all his paperwork on Lydia's desk. He then expected it to disappear. She supposed the mess cooperated by disappearing for him for years, first with help from his mother and now with Lydia's elbow grease.

"New client? Who?" Lydia asked. Clients seldom came to the office. The D'Angelos apparently always met them somewhere dark so they could pour out their tales of woe and ask for the services of a private eye discreetly. Lydia was disappointed when she discovered her only contact with most of their cases was going to be through the reports and expense spreadsheets.

"Robert Carroll. A guy who thinks his wife is unfaithful."

"He's got love troubles, huh?" Besides corporate clients, those with matrimonial troubles appeared to bring in the most business for the D'Angelos. She thought it was nice that the high divorce rate was at least good for somebody.

Frankie sighed. "Doesn't everyone?" Lydia shot Frankie a speculative glance. She wondered if he had some dark love affair in his background that ruined him for the fair sex. The fact that neither Leo nor Frankie ever seemed to have a date was quite intriguing. She supposed they could be gay, which would explain a lot. She doubted that homosexuality was on Mama D'Angelo's approved list of lifestyle choices, so they would both have to be locked in a deep, dark closet.

"Sometimes it's trouble with money," Lydia said, sipping her coffee from a giant mug that looked like a curvy Hollywood starlet from the 1950s. The starlet's large red lips were beginning to rub off from repeated washings, but this just added to the mug's charm.

"And sometimes it's both. Usually, they're trying to protect their assets in a divorce settlement."

Lydia could see this job could lead to permanent disillusionment with the married state, and she hoped it wouldn't happen to her.

She did her best in the next hour to straighten the office and make it look less gross, even digging out a can of furniture polish. She found it satisfying to wipe surfaces clean and get a big smear of black dust on her cloth. She washed the cups in the sink, then blasted through the filing in record time. The office now qualified as neat, but it still looked dingy. There was only so much she could do with what she was given. The beat-up desks looked no better without their layer of papers, but at least they weren't dusty and covered with stained coffee mugs.

Since a client was coming, Lydia was glad that she'd dressed up for the day. She was wearing a beautiful off-white blouse with billowing poet sleeves, and soft red velvet pants. The outfit looked odd when paired with snow boots, but now in the office, wearing red embroidered Chinese slippers, she looked quite elegant.

Mr. Carroll showed up late. He looked around the office and frowned. Lydia smiled to herself when she remembered how her expectations of a private eye's office had not matched her first impressions of the D'Angelos' place. She expected a dark, smoky office with a dash of danger, just like in those Humphrey Bogart movies. The only similarity between the two that she could see was dimness. In Bogart's office, it added a touch of intrigue. At the D'Angelos', the darkness made it difficult for Lydia to do the filing without turning on all the lights.

Then Mr. Carroll shot Lydia a suspicious glance, as if she was going to be standing up to defend the virtue of the fairer sex. She decided her best bet was to keep her head down and look busy. Her latest project was an attempt to drag the D'Angelos into the twenty-first century by inputting their Rolodex files into the computer. She was amazed how reliant they were on scraps of paper, and she hoped this would help them contact a few of their clients about repeat business.

The D'Angelos began to interview Mr. Carroll over Leo's desk, speaking in hushed tones, as if discussing funeral arrangements. "My wife normally spends the day doing the shopping and running errands. But lately there's been no food in the house, and I've come home before her three times."

Lydia would have been more outraged on behalf of all women, especially for Mrs. Carroll, who was perhaps taking a well-earned break, if Mr. Carroll hadn't sounded so upset. He obviously loved his wife, and the suspicion that she had taken up with another man was driving him crazy. Lydia wondered what he would do if he found out it was true. She hoped they would get counseling, but she guessed they would probably get a divorce. She wondered how many of the D'Angelos' clients had ever resorted to murder. Some people could not control their jealous rages. She wondered if Marie'd had trouble with a jealous and abusive boyfriend but had not told anyone about it. So much about her death still puzzled Lydia.

After the D'Angelos had agreed to follow Mrs. Carroll for a few days, and deliver any evidence they collected to her husband, they signed a quick contract. Mr. Carroll shook hands with them and left quickly, as if he was afraid his wife was tracking his movements.

Frowning, Frankie studied the photograph Mr. Carroll had left. "She's a real beauty." Lydia sneaked a peek. Mrs. Carroll was a blonde and looked like she had had a lot of work done. Her eyes were beginning to look a little stretched, and it wasn't natural to have no lines at all on her face.

"Then you won't mind taking the first shift, huh?" Leo said with a smirk.

"Oh, all right," Frankie said. "She shouldn't suspect a thing."

Leo shook his head. "Don't forget to keep your eyes open. Problems can come up everywhere." Leo turned to Lydia. "We were once on a routine job, tracing a birth mother. We neglected to bring any disguises, and the woman spotted us following her. She went all crazy, thinking we were sent by her parole officer, and she stabbed Frankie with a Swiss army knife. It was ugly."

Leo was always full of doom and gloom, and pretty depressing to be around. The worst part was that most of his predictions came true.

"I still have the scar," Frankie said cheerfully, looking at Lydia. "It reminds me to keep back a safe distance and change disguises if I think I've been spotted." Frankie usually looked on the bright side of every situation, and Lydia was glad to see him acting normally. Frankie had been strangely moody lately, thereby resembling his brother, Leo, more than his usual sunny self.

"It sounds exciting," Lydia said. "I wouldn't mind trying a stakeout one of these days." It certainly couldn't be duller than in-putting client data.

Leo frowned. "Maybe someday. But we use only trained detectives for this kind of work."

Lydia shrugged. She knew she would be soon sorting out receipts for the case and printing out the photographs he brought back. Maybe someday they would trust her to do it on her own.

The D'Angelos left at five o'clock, as usual. Lydia took advantage of their absence to close up early. She had an appointment with Marie's address book.

Chapter 10

Lydia sat down at her dining room table to study Marie's weekly planner and photographs. The black leather book was slim and the small squares for each day were filled with Marie's ungainly scrawl. The handwriting was too difficult to decipher at first glance, so she set aside the book and skipped to the fun part—the photos.

Marie's party the previous year had been a blast. Marie'd had a gift for collecting creative friends and then inspiring them to use their talents for her birthday. A designer friend decked out her apartment to resemble a giant red silk tent. It looked like it belonged more in the desert than in Brooklyn. A florist buddy of hers covered every available surface with fragrant rose petals. A baker friend made dozens of adorable cupcakes with portraits of Marie on them. Georgia Rae's band had played, and although the place was packed with people, everyone danced the night away.

Lydia recognized most of the people in the photos, but she set aside a few pictures of some she had never seen before. She would have to ask Emily or Georgia to help her in identifying them. Lydia found a cute picture of Marie, Georgia, Emily, and herself hamming it up for the camera and she decided to keep it. She needed to remember the good times. In the photos, Lydia wore an off-the-shoulder turquoise prom dress from the 1950s, and Marie wore one of her signature sheath dresses in a deep orange, which made her look tall and elegant. Lydia missed her. She had been so young and vibrant, and her death was a horrible tragedy. Who might have killed Marie? A jealous lover, a disgruntled fellow photographer, or a dissatisfied client: None of the possibilities seemed likely.

She turned back to Marie's weekly planner, a two-year calendar; the pages contained both the previous year and the coming one. Lydia turned to the month of January and looked down the page. She noted sadly that Marie had planned to go to her show on Thursday. She wished today were her opening again and Marie had arrived safe. Lydia would have given anything to have that day back and have everything go right this time.

She managed to read through Marie's other recent appointments, but she understood very few of them. There were a few notes about *Beauty* magazine and *Vogue,* likely photo shoots that Marie was now going to miss. Her career had really been taking off, and Lydia was saddened that she wasn't going to see all her work come to fruition. There was a dentist appointment still to come, and a trip to Iceland that she would never get to go on. Lydia wondered how long it took before all traces of a person disappeared. Perhaps it was when there were no longer events where people expected someone's presence, and that person began to cease to exist even in memory.

At the back of the planner was an address book with a few phone numbers. Lydia copied them down dutifully in her own notebook. Jeanne Goldberg, the editor of *Beauty* magazine, the creative director of an ad agency, and the head of another magazine. She was disappointed to find so few. Probably the bulk of Marie's numbers were in her cell phone, and Lydia wondered what had happened to it. In the notes section was a list of strange numbers that were too long to be phone numbers, but she couldn't identify what they were for. Possibly they were software ID numbers, but their true purpose had been lost when Marie died. Lydia copied them down just in case.

She resolved to turn Marie's planner over to Romero but decided to keep the photographs. The memories were still too fresh and painful. Her friends looked carefree—and a little drunk. If Romero asked for the photos, she would give them to him, but until that time they would stay with her.

Remembering that she had promised Marie's mother she would make some calls about the memorial service, she dialed each number listed. She reached the voice mails of the managing editor at *Beauty* magazine and Marie's other clients. None of them was picking up the phone late in the day, but she left each of them the details of the memorial service anyway.

Once her task was done, she sat at the table, staring at the photographs and planner. She wished she could make them give up their secrets and tell her why this terrible tragedy had happened to Marie. Who were her enemies? Who wanted to ruin Lydia's photo career? None of it made sense. She worried again about her other models. She called Georgia and Emily quickly and was relieved to reach them.

Emily acted like she was crazy to worry. "It was probably an isolated incident."

"But what if it isn't?" She wanted to tell Emily about how Marie had been posed, but she couldn't. She was afraid that Marie's murder was just the beginning.

"The neighborhood is very safe," Emily said, sounding distracted. "Marie wouldn't want you to stress out and forget to enjoy life."

Emily was right about Marie. Marie had loved life, and had had only disdain for people who wasted it living out their days in fear. But sometimes a little healthy fear kept you from getting killed.

"Marie's mom said you dropped by. Did you get something to read?"

Lydia didn't want to admit defeat. "Sure. I'm all set."

"I wish the rest were as organized as you. I'm going crazy trying to pin everyone down. I'd love to get someone she worked with to speak."

"I left messages for some of them. When they call me, I'll ask them."

"Could you? That would be great." Emily sounded breathy and artificial, like a cheerleader again. She didn't sound very upset about Marie's death. Maybe she was channeling her grief into planning the memorial service.

"Just remember to take care of yourself, okay?" Lydia reminded her. Emily got on her nerves sometimes, but she wanted her to stay alive and annoy her for years to come.

Chapter 11

Lydia woke up fuzzy-headed the next day and peered at her ringing alarm clock. The time was 8:00 A.M. She had tossed and turned all night, thinking about Marie. The radiators in her apartment were barely functioning, and even wearing lots of layers and piling on stacks of blankets, she was still chilled.

After showering in record time, since the water never got hotter than lukewarm, she first dried her hair and then turned the dryer on her feet to thaw them out. Luckily, she had laid out her outfit carefully on a chair the night before. She pulled on a pair of black fishnet stockings, wiggled into a denim skirt, and tossed on an Icelandic sweater, her fuzzy boots, and her cape.

Outside, the air smelled cold and fresh, and just a little bit salty. The wind was coming from the ocean. She sometimes forgot how close they were to the water, and then she would smell the sea or spot a seagull sailing overhead. The snow looked like a congealed gray mass, with only a skinny shoveled path down the middle of the sidewalk. She dropped an envelope, which was addressed to Romero and contained Marie's planner, into a mailbox dripping with icicles. Her conscience clear, she ducked into the closest coffee shop. She emerged with a steaming hot cup and a muffin, planning to eat her breakfast at work.

When Lydia arrived at the office, the only D'Angelo there was Mama. She was sitting at Lydia's desk, using the phone. Mama almost never came around. She was too busy running her busy restaurant. Besides, her sons were over at her restaurant for almost every meal, so she had no need to come over to see them.

Mama D'Angelo quickly hung up the phone when Lydia entered and folded her hands in front of her on the desk. "Good morning, Lydia! You look frozen!"

Lydia set her bag down wearily. She had hoped that the office would be quiet so she could catch up on some personal work in peace. "There's some trouble with the heat in my building."

"Hmm. I know someone who could speak to your landlord and get that taken care of," Mama said with a frown.

Lydia imagined her landlord getting a call from a mobster named Guido or something, and the thought made her smile. "That's okay. I'm going to call the housing department. That usually sets him straight for a couple of weeks at least."

Mama shrugged. "What do my sons have you working on anyway?"

"This and that," Lydia said. "Billing, filing."

Mama looked around the office, unimpressed. She made it quite clear that she believed her deceased husband and now her sons didn't really work for a living at the detective agency, but had somehow hoodwinked everyone into believing that they did. Mama got up out of the desk chair and stepped over to the coffeemaker. She tsk-tsked when she saw it was empty and began to make a new pot.

Lydia sorted the mail and tossed out offers for exotic vacations, credit cards, and new furniture. She tossed the bills into her in-box.

Mama D'Angelo stood there watching the coffeemaker drip. Lydia had never seen Mama stand still for so long, so she knew something was wrong. "Are you okay?"

Mama turned around and folded her arms across her chest. "I'm worried about my Frankie."

Lydia was mystified. "Frankie? Is he sick?"

"Yes," Mama said venomously. "Sick in the heart, sick in the head. What do you know about this computer dating?"

"Frankie is dating someone?"

Mama began to pace around the small office angrily. Papers flew off Lydia's desk in her wake. "He put his picture up on a Web site and he has begun to go out with women. Strange women. They're not Italian. They're *puttane*!"

"Have you met any of them?" Lydia collected her papers from the floor and had the strange sensation of falling down a rabbit hole. She often felt like she was missing a piece of the puzzle when she dealt with the D'Angelos.

"No! I wouldn't let some whore in my house," Mama said, outraged.

Lydia found a roll of Life Savers in her desk drawer and popped one in her mouth. She counted to ten. "How do you know they're so awful, then?"

"A mother knows these things. One of them is going to get her claws into my son. He'll start giving her money and be left penniless and with a broken heart." Mama watched a lot of soap operas, but she sounded truly upset. Lydia was starting to get a clearer picture of why the D'Angelo brothers never dated anyone. Supposedly, Leo had been married and divorced, but as far as she knew, Frankie had never had a serious relationship. Their mother was beyond controlling. But it was none of Lydia's business.

Mama D'Angelo grabbed Lydia's arm. She was strong from kneading all that pizza dough. "You have to help me, Lydia.'

Mama's garlic breath was overpowering. When Mama let go to pace around the office, Lydia edged around her desk, out of reach.

"What do you want me to do? Frankie is a grown man." Grown men usually gave up the *ie* at the end of their names, but as her boss, Frankie definitely did qualify as an adult.

"I want you to keep your eyes open," Mama hissed. "You are good at observing things. I must be at the restaurant all day, but you see what goes on here. Tell me if he meets someone."

Lydia didn't like the idea of spying on Frankie for Mama. She was caught in a bind, though. If she displeased their mother for any reason, Frankie and Leo would be mad at her. But if they knew she was reporting their movements to Mama, they would probably be mad at her, as well.

Mama could see the indecision on her face, and she pounced. "There is no need to tell me everything. My fondest hope is that he meets a nice girl and settles down. But I want to be there to help him from making a big mistake, you understand? No matter how old he is, I am still his mother."

Lydia decided her best bet would be to agree to spy on Frankie and possibly get some pastries out of the deal. But she wouldn't call and report anything to Mama unless it seemed like something she should really know. If Frankie brought a perfectly nice woman into the office, Lydia would respect their privacy. But if he hooked up with some kind of Cruella de Vil, she would alert Mama so she could swoop down and protect her baby chick.

Lydia nodded and Mama beamed. She enveloped Lydia in a suffocating hug as Lydia's cell phone began to tweet somewhere in the purse under her desk. Despite the fact that the D'Angelos frowned on her taking personal calls at work, Lydia used the phone as an excuse to step away from Mama's embrace and fished it out. Mama D'Angelo, satisfied by Lydia's agreement to spy, waved and left, leaving Lydia to answer the call.

The number was unfamiliar on the screen. "I'm trying to reach Lydia McKenzie. This is Jeanne Goldberg from *Beauty* magazine." Jeanne had hardly waited for Lydia to say hello. Her voice was deep and authoritative.

"This is Lydia. Did you have any questions about Marie's service?"

"Not at all. I need to speak to you immediately about another matter. I am currently driving over the Williamsburg Bridge. Where do you live?"

"I'm at work," Lydia stammered. She was not dressed to speak with the editor of a beauty magazine. She did not have on lipstick or mascara, and she felt like a windblown mess after her trek to work. But she owed it to Marie's family to try to convince Jeanne to speak at the service.

"Give my driver your address," Jeanne ordered.

She apparently handed her phone to her driver, because a man with a thick Brooklyn accent spoke next.

Lydia bowed to the inevitable and gave the driver directions. "Do you know where Leonard and Metropolitan avenues intersect?" But she wondered what Jeanne wanted. She could be looking for photographers. Lydia had never been particularly interested in shooting fashion, preferring to keep her art out of the commercial realm, but a well-paid gig at a magazine could take care of all her bills and make it unnecessary to deal with the D'Angelos' soap opera.

She couldn't figure out why Jeanne would rush over the Williamsburg Bridge first thing in the morning to speak to her. She got Lydia's contact information when she had called about the service, but she said that wasn't what she wanted to speak about. Lydia wondered if she had seen something suspicious before Marie had died, and didn't know whom to tell. If that was why she was coming, Lydia would tell her that she should go straight to the police.

She guessed that she had about ten minutes before Jeanne came in the door. She dug in her purse and found a lip gloss and a dull eyebrow pencil. They would have to do. She washed her face in the bathroom, brushed her hair, and applied makeup. Feeling slightly more presentable, she returned to her desk to wait.

Nothing could have prepared her for Jeanne Goldberg, though. The door opened with a bang, revealing a small woman in a perfectly tailored Prada suit. Her heels were impossibly high, and she strode in surrounded by a cloud of exotic French perfume. She had killer cheekbones and black hair, with a streak of white framing the left side of her face. Jeanne scanned the D'Angelos' office with a look of disdain and then turned her gaze on Lydia. Lydia straightened in her chair and met her eyes squarely.

"What is all this about Marie dying?" Jeanne asked imperiously. Her tone implied that Marie's death was a great inconvenience to her, and all Marie's fault.

"She was murdered," Lydia began. "Didn't you see the news?"

Jeanne waved her hand. "I only read magazines. No time for current events. Are you in charge of her papers?"

"What do you mean?"

Jeanne's red lips twisted. "Marie was a very naughty girl, and she had some photographs of mine that I need back."

"I don't know what you mean. . . ." Lydia began, confused.

"C'mon, girl. Don't waste my time. If you think I'm going to give you the same deal I gave Marie, you've got another thing coming. I have no time for blackmail. Hand it over."

"Marie was no blackmailer. . . ." Lydia rose up out of her chair indignantly.

"You didn't know her very well, did you?" Jeanne's thin smile looked ominous. "If you don't have her papers, then tell me who does."

Lydia imagined Jeanne bursting into Marie's apartment and ordering Marie's mother around. Marie's mom certainly did not need that kind of aggravation. Lydia had to find a way to divert her. "I'll find what you need."

"I guess I'll have to trust you." Jeanne looked around the office, noting the decor for perhaps the first time. She grimaced at the old gray carpet and frowned at the old stained desks. Then Lydia saw Jeanne focus on one of her photographs on the wall. It was the recreation of the murder of a woman who had been shot in the chest and left in an alleyway in 1985. Georgia Rae had been the model. "What's that?"

"That's one of my photographs." Lydia tried not to sound too proud.

"You took that?" Jeanne moved closer to examine the print. Lydia held her a breath for a moment, telling herself she didn't care if Jeanne liked it or not. She had worked hard to get the right look for the alley, and had removed anything that looked like it had been manufactured after the 1980s. She had tried to make the murder scene look as historically accurate as possible, and found her knowledge of vintage clothing useful.

Jeanne pivoted away with a sniff. "It's too bad corpses are very two years ago, or we could use you for a spread in *Beauty*."

Lydia knew right then that it wouldn't matter if Jeanne offered her a million dollars; she never in her life wanted to work for someone like her. Jeanne put one of her business cards down on Lydia's desk with a snap. "Call me when you know where her papers are."

Lydia left the card untouched and watched as Jeanne swept from the room, leaving the scent of her perfume behind her like a bad memory.

Chapter 12

The caffeine in her system was long gone, and Lydia wanted only to go home and crash. Georgia called and asked her to come along to hear a band, but she told her there was no way she could make it. Nirvana tonight would be a bowl of tomato soup and melted-cheese sandwiches. She stopped for supplies at a Korean grocery on the way home. The wind was cold and biting and sneaked through every layer. She wished she had money and could afford to fly somewhere warm in the wintertime. Someplace with white sand beaches and endless sunshine would be perfect, she thought as she sidestepped some dog poop that was probably going to be frozen on the sidewalk until the spring thaw.

At home, she started her tomato soup warming on the stove and her cheesy bread cooking in the broiler. She changed into men's red tartan flannel pajamas and puttered around the house. Already the day was fading from her mind—until her cell phone tweeted, insistent and loud in the kitchen. She picked it up and looked at the screen. Jacques Bulan was calling. She squashed the urge to throw the phone against the fridge. It would only hurt the phone and Bulan would never know. Her curiosity got the better of her.

She answered the phone.

Jacques was stone-cold sober, which was the first surprise. "A collector is really excited about your work and wants to meet you tonight."

Lydia couldn't help but wail, "Tonight?"

"He's only in town one night. Come over as soon as you can." Lydia looked longingly at her tomato soup steaming on the stove. As much as she hated Jacques, she couldn't pass up a possible sale.

"I'll be there in fifteen minutes." She wolfed down the soup, just lukewarm, and ate her sandwiches while dashing about getting dressed again. It was a real juggling act and it was a miracle she got only one spot of grease on her sweater. Suede pants, high-heeled boots, a turtleneck sweater, and a pair of crazy chandelier earrings completed her outfit. She dabbed on some mascara while she threw all her dirty dishes in the sink. Then she shrugged on her coat and ran out the door. As soon as she shut it, she realized she had left her phone on the counter. She opened the door again, grabbed her phone, and was on her way. But now she was really late.

The gallery wasn't far from her apartment, but the cold night air and the thin layer of snow made it feel much farther. She set off as quickly as she could, wishing she had worn her furry boots instead. The sidewalk was slippery and her high-heeled boots had barely any traction.

She never worried much about the crime rate in the neighborhood and had managed to avoid getting mugged so far. Some of her friends had not been so lucky. Marie's murder and the self-defense class made her feel paranoid. She imagined something moving on every dark street corner, and wished she had the cash to take a car service.

Lydia was surprised to find the simple metal door to the Bulan Gallery ajar. Usually, Jacques made everyone wait outside the locked door until he came to the front, but he had thoughtfully left it open for once. Lydia stepped inside the simple brick building and shut the door behind her.

The gallery space was dark and oddly quiet. She pushed ahead before the boulder-size lump in her throat threatened to choke her. Just a few days ago, the gallery had been filled with her friends. She wished her show had turned out differently, and it made her sick when she thought of poor Marie and her senseless death. She moved quickly through the room, heading toward Jacques's office.

"Jacques? It's Lydia," she called out. There was no answer. She hoped Jacques hadn't drunk himself into a stupor again. She knew alcoholism was a disease, but she found it hard to be sympathetic with someone who had few, if any, desirable characteristics. She heaved a sigh and entered his office. She was here to meet or find out about someone interested in her work, and it was her first real break in awhile. If they bought one or two pieces, she would be in a much healthier place financially.

The office was dark and quiet, too. She started to back out, when her eyes suddenly adjusted to the darkness and she spotted someone sitting in the office chair in the dim light.

"Jacques?" she said tentatively, wondering if he was asleep or had passed out. He didn't answer. She wondered for a moment if she should turn around and go home and wait until he was conscious. But something didn't feel right. The room was too still. Lydia fumbled along the wall until she found the light switch. She flipped it on and gasped when she saw what a mess his office was. Papers were strewn everywhere. Artwork had been ripped from the walls, their frames torn and twisted and their glass broken. A blue-and-white-patterned vase of Jacques's lay in pieces on the floor.

She turned to look at the person at the desk. It was Jacques. He was slumped forward, with his face on his mahogany desk. She gasped, afraid that someone who disliked him more than she did had finally killed him.

Chapter 13

Dialing a phone with shaking hands wasn't easy. Luckily, Lydia needed to dial only three numbers: 911.

"I think I just found a dead body," Lydia said with a trembling voice.

"A dead body? What is your location?" The dispatcher was so cool, she sounded bored.

Lydia gave the address. She knew it by heart, after sending out hundreds of invitations for her show. That seemed so long ago.

"Did you feel for a pulse?"

"Uh, no." Lydia had had no desire to touch Jacques when he was alive, and she had even less desire to do so now that he was dead. But this was an emergency. She reached over and grasped his pale wrist with one hand. There was a faint pulse.

"He's alive," Lydia said. She felt almost giddy with relief. "But he's been viciously attacked, and his gallery was ransacked."

The dispatcher promised to send an ambulance right away. Lydia hung up, wondering why Jacques had been a target. Was it just a simple robbery? Considering the state of his finances, she doubted there was much cash lying around. Of course, robbers wouldn't have known that. But what if they'd been after something else?

Suddenly, she remembered that Jacques had said he was going to introduce her to a collector. Had the collector never shown up? She decided to take a look around while she was waiting for the ambulance and the cops to arrive.

His office was a wreck, and most of the papers strewn about were from artists begging him to show their work. Lydia's heart went out to them, but she wondered if they knew how lucky they were to have avoided showing at Bulan.

The bathroom door was closed. Lydia approached it with caution, suddenly fearful that the attacker was still hanging around. But she had to make sure that there wasn't another victim lying somewhere, bleeding to death. She slowly put her hand on the doorknob and turned it. The bathroom looked the same as always. The bathtub was filled with paintings, and Jacques had never bothered to paint the Sheetrock walls. He put his money and resources into the things his clients would see and skimped on the rest.

There were no other doors or dark corners for an attacker to hide in. She wondered if there was a possible clue to the collector's identity on Jacques's desk. She remembered he had a large calendar on the desktop that he doodled on while he spoke on the phone. Unfortunately, he was lying facedown on the calendar. It could be detrimental to his health to move him and take a peek, and even worse, she might get caught.

On the floor by the desk was a pile of portfolio books from all the gallery's artists. The thief must have taken them off the bookshelf and thrown them all down on the ground. A violent pig. Lydia suddenly remembered her portfolio book. It contained xeroxed pictures of all her photographs from the series. Lydia pushed through the pile with her foot but couldn't see it anywhere. She knelt down and methodically went through all the books, but she still didn't see it. It didn't feel right. Surely he would have taken her book out if he planned to meet with someone about her work.

Lydia stood up, wondering if someone posing as a collector could have done this to Jacques. If he thought he was about to make a big sale, he would have been blind with greed. He would never have seen it coming. If the attacker had been the same one as Marie's killer, he wasn't finished yet. He had stolen Lydia's book of photographs, and she got nauseated thinking what a killer could do with it.

Jacques stirred and lifted up his head groggily.

"Oh, my head," he moaned. He opened his eyes and looked straight at Lydia. "Why you—" His eyes narrowed. "You hit me!"

Lydia shook her head. "I didn't touch you. I came over because you called me, and I found your head planted on the table. Don't you remember what happened?"

"I was talking to . . ." he began, and winced. "I can't remember his name."

"The collector?" she prompted.

"Right, right. And he picked out your book and said he wanted to meet you," Jacques said, and frowned. "I tried to interest him in some of my other artists whose work is at the gallery, but he insisted on meeting you." Lydia just bet he'd been discouraging. She was starting to wish the blow had been fatal. The world would probably have been better off without him.

The front door opened with a bang, and Romero and Wong strode into the gallery. Romero stopped when he saw Lydia and frowned. "What are you doing here?"

"He called and told me to come over. . . ." she began.

"I've been viciously robbed, and this would never have happened without her," Jacques said at the same time.

"Why you—" Lydia sputtered. She'd tried to help, and now he was doing his best to get her arrested. She wondered if he could have injured himself on purpose. He would have to be a talented contortionist if he had.

Romero held up his hands. "Quiet down, both of you." He turned to Jacques. "Mr. Bulan, can you tell me what happened this evening?"

Jacques nodded and then clutched his head in pain. "A man was here tonight who told me he collected photographs. He said he was interested in Lydia's work and wanted to meet her. I called her and she came over. He must have hit me on the head. . . ."

"And he stole my book, which has copies of all the photographs in the series."

Romero took out a notebook from his pocket. "Describe the man for me."

Jacques began to describe him, but he sounded like any white guy in his thirties who lived in Williamsburg. He had no particularly distinguishing characteristics, no visible tattoo or scar. She wondered if he was describing Marie's killer, or if this had been the work of a random sicko who had found out the connection between Lydia's work and Marie's death and wanted to make a splash.

The EMTs arrived, interrupting the interrogation. They gently pushed the detectives away and proceeded to give Jacques a thorough examination. Romero guided Lydia into the main gallery space. Her head was swimming with fatigue. The lights were on in the space, and she saw for the first time that the attacker had sprayed her photos with red paint.

Lydia stumbled, and Romero reached out to catch her before she fell. It took her a minute before she could step away and recover her voice. "Oh my God. How awful."

"It'll wash off."

The stain would never wash out, not in her mind. She could never look again at the photographs without seeing the red and feeling sad. "I don't want anyone else to die. I need to take them down and close the show."

"That's probably a good idea."

She tried for a moment to see them as he probably did, tawdry and violent exercises that had brought evil down upon her friends. "I'll take them down tomorrow."

Her show was over, but she wasn't so sure that the killer was finished.

Chapter 14

Lydia stopped in the doorway of D'Angelos' office, alert. Something felt out of place. Something felt off. Then it hit her. The office just didn't feel right without a big guy with his feet up on the desk reading the newspaper. "Where's Frankie?"

"Shopping," Leo said, disgusted, "with his girlfriend." Lydia looked at him blankly for a moment and then she remembered the computer dating service. She luckily knew nothing about the girlfriend, so she couldn't rat him out and tell Mama D'Angelo anything about her. She guessed love did strange things to a guy, because Lydia had never known Frankie to shop for anything other than food. She hoped he was happy. Maybe he could find a way to set up Leo, too, and get him out of the dumps.

Her phone tweeted, indicating that she had a message, and she dug around in her purse, trying to find it. Instead of her phone, her hand closed over a packet of photographs, the photos from Marie's party. She looked over at Leo furtively, but he wasn't paying any attention to her. He was going to get carpal tunnel syndrome if he didn't stop hunching over his computer like that.

She missed Marie. Maybe just a quick glance at her photos would satisfy her. She opened up the sleeve and slipped out the pictures. She paged through them until she came to a shot of two women kissing. She did not remember seeing it before. Maybe it had stuck to another, or maybe she'd been too focused on photos of her friends. The flash on the camera had illuminated the women harshly—not one of Marie's better efforts. It was no social, polite kiss. Their lips were locked together like those of passionate lovers. One of the women had pale blond curly hair, and Lydia did not recognize her. The other woman had black hair with a white streak, and was none other than Jeanne from *Beauty* magazine.

Lydia stared at the photo in her hand, wondering if this could have been the secret that Marie had known about Jeanne. The fashion world appeared, at face value, to be inclusive and unconcerned with sexuality, but perhaps a magazine like *Beauty* was more conservative. If Jeanne thought her career might be ruined or hurt by gossip about her sexual preferences, and Marie had stumbled upon her secret, could Jeanne have killed Marie to keep it from getting out?

Lydia's mind reeled over the possibilities. She had no idea what to think. She decided that she wouldn't share the photograph with Romero unless she gathered more evidence that it was tied to the murder. Meanwhile, the photograph gave Lydia an unexpected leverage with Jeanne. After listening to her message, a voice mail from Georgia, who was just checking in, she dug up Jeanne's phone number and left her a clear, concise message. She hung up, satisfied. If Jeanne came to Marie's funeral, Lydia would know that she had taken the bait.

She could not ignore the stack of junk mail and bills on her desk any longer, so she got back to work.

At the end of the day, she stood up and stretched her aching back. Her desk looked slightly better, and the D'Angelos' client list now existed in a digital form. Unfortunately, the evening ahead contained a chore she wasn't anxious to do. She had to go to the Bulan Gallery and take her show down, just one heartbreaking week after she had hung it.

Lydia had dreamed about having a New York show from the first moment she arrived in the city. Her photo style had been gradually taking shape ever since. She had absorbed various influences as she honed her craft. Slowly, she had found her voice and vision, and created a cohesive body of work. She'd been in the occasional group show, where one of her photographs was hung out of context and was usually overlooked in the midst of an eclectic mix of work. But the solo show of her dreams had been beyond her reach for years. When Jacques offered to show her prints, it felt at first like her career was made. She'd had no idea what the consequences would be for showing her photos.

The Williamsburg art community was still suffering growing pains. Although it felt like a new gallery opened every couple of months, other galleries had packed up and moved back to Manhattan. Chelsea provided more foot traffic, and the rents were starting to be comparable. But a show was a show, and Lydia had sincerely hoped it would lead to bigger and better things.

A forlorn Lydia rang the bell at the Bulan Gallery. There was no answer. She had made an appointment with Jacques earlier that day, so he knew she was coming. Lydia rang again, wondering with concern if he'd had a relapse.

Finally, Jacques opened the door with a French curse. He had an artistic white silk scarf wrapped around his head like a bandage and a ferocious frown on his face. He was carrying a bottle of red wine in one hand. Without a word, he turned and left the door open behind him. This'll be fun, she thought to herself as she pushed her way inside. Jacques's attitude reminded her of an exalted and petulant diva's. Except divas, for the most part, were talented, or no one would put up with their posturing. She rued the day that she had signed on with Jacques. He was an unreliable drunk, and somehow everything felt like it was his fault.

Lydia followed him into the main gallery space, averting her eyes from the office, where he had been attacked. Although her photographs had been wiped clean, she still felt as if she could see the red paint staining them. She had worked hard on her portfolio, but the killer had managed to spoil her pride in her art, and her enjoyment of what should have been the evening of her life.

Jacques uncorked a bottle of wine with his teeth and took a swig. He swallowed loudly and held out the bottle to Lydia. She shook her head. She did not have any desire to share saliva with Jacques. She also needed all her wits about her to pack up the show. But she doubted that drinking and a bump on the head would mix well, either. "Aren't you worried about a concussion?"

"It's the only thing for the pain. Although why he went for me and not you, I do not understand," Jacques said with a sneer, and plunked himself down in a chair to watch her take down the show on her own. The only thing to do was pack up as quickly as possible and get out.

Lydia stepped back into his storeroom to retrieve the boxes and bubble wrap she'd used to protect the prints on the way to the show. She trudged back into the gallery and set the boxes down in the middle of the floor. Every piece needed to be wrapped and packed. The task was both depressing and daunting. She had hoped to sell a few of the prints and have a lot less to haul home, but no collectors had come calling, begging for the chance to buy one.

With Jacques's accusing eyes boring into her back, Lydia took down the first photograph and wrapped it carefully in bubble wrap. The photograph re-created the deaths of two middle-aged hookers, who had been strangled and left half-clothed on a bare mattress on the floor in 1988. Lydia had counteracted the unintentional sexiness of the photograph with stark and unrelenting light. Every flaw was exposed, and she'd provided examples of lives spent in quiet desperation: a crack pipe, stained clothing, and sex toys. Both women wore tangled wigs and had thick, smeared makeup, which obscured Lydia's and Emily's identities as the models. Posing and taking the picture had been difficult, but Marie had helped her snap the final shot.

Lydia carefully taped the bubble wrap and set the photograph in a box. She stood up and took another print down from the wall. The next was one she called *Jane Doe Number 5.* She was a young kid from the sticks who had come into the big city and fallen prey to one of the evil people who cruise bus stations looking for lost souls. Jane Doe died from poisoned heroin, and her body had been dumped unceremoniously on a trash heap in an alley. They estimated that she was fifteen or sixteen when she died, and as she tried to wrap the print as quickly as possible, Lydia wondered why her family had never come forward to claim her. Jenny Powers, from her art-critique group, had posed for the photograph, and her wholesome young face had made her a believable teen. Lydia had taken the photograph in an alley, giving the hint of a rat by placing a rubber one in a trash-filled corner. She had loved creating the atmospheres and dressing the victims in interesting colors. Some of the nuances were lost in black and white, but the interesting filmic look she'd achieved with black and white made it well worth it.

Lydia put the bundle into the box, then moved on to the next. She knew she was mooning over each print and going slower than she probably should be. She wasn't sure when the photographs would hang together again. It felt almost like she was wishing each one good-bye. She heard Jacques put his wine bottle on the desk with a thud. She took the next print down at a slightly faster speed. She wanted to get away from the oppressive atmosphere of the gallery as soon as she could, but she had to be careful not to scratch or break the glass on any of her prints.

"I never liked your work, you know. It's too garish and gruesome for my tastes." Jacques's words were slurred, but they still burrowed beneath her skin like poisonous darts.

Lydia whirled around and glared at Jacques. She was tired of his nastiness. It didn't matter anymore if they got along. Their business relationship was officially over. "Then why did you hang it on your walls? You probably get fifty inquiries a week from desperate artists."

Jacques shrugged. "I thought the murder thing might get some attention and help me move some pieces. I tried to get that guy who photographs executions in the Middle East, but he already has a gallery in Chelsea."

Lydia felt her eyes fill with tears. She did not want this jerk to see her cry. He was trying to hurt her, and she wanted him to see that she was strong and confident. Only with her first show lying in ruins around her, and one of her friends murdered, she felt completely insecure. Lydia took down another print, wrapped it in bubble wrap, and willed herself to pack faster.

Jacques wasn't finished, though. He uncorked another bottle and took a swig. "I decided to take a chance on you, despite the fact that you have no track record. And what's the thanks I get? I'm left with an aching head, an empty space, and not a single sale."

Good, Lydia thought to herself. I hope you're completely ruined. I hope you end up in a homeless shelter. Jacques was a truly hateful person, and she wished nothing but cloudy days, broken-down cars, and migraine headaches for him.

Jacques's doorbell rang. He made no move to answer it. The bell rang again and again, signaling that whoever was at the door did not intend to give up. Lydia ignored it the best she could. She had filled one box and was moving on to the next. Jacques's bad business practices were no business of hers anymore. At last, Jacques finally lurched out of his chair, swearing loudly.

"Keep your shirt on—I'm coming." He tottered to the door and flung it open. An elderly man pushed past him. "Oh, you. You have no right to come in here."

"I have every right," the man said in a heavy Polish accent. He was wearing a down parka, black pleated slacks and wing-tipped shoes. "This property belongs to me."

"That doesn't mean you can barge right in. Can't you see I'm in the middle of something?"

The landlord looked over at Lydia with mild curiosity. Lydia quickly put her head back down and concentrated on packing up her last four prints.

"Here is your eviction notice. You have not paid rent for three months. I want you out by the end of the week."

"You've been trying to ruin me since I first opened this place. I should sue you!" Jacques shrieked. His French accent had disappeared and had been replaced by a flat midwestern twang. She felt a pang of sympathy for him. He was a fraud, but he was also in big trouble.

"You are welcome to try to bring a suit against me, but you know you will be laughed out of the court. I am a fair and honest landlord. You don't have a leg to stand on right now. Either pay me my money or get out."

Jacques continued to splutter, but he undoubtedly didn't have the money to pay. Lydia wondered what would have happened if he had sold some of her pieces. He probably would have kept the cash to pay his bills, and cheated her out of her rightful share. She quickly suppressed any bubbling sympathetic feelings she had for him.

Lydia wrapped up the last piece and slipped it into the box. The two boxes were heavy, but she found the strength necessary to drag them both toward the door. The landlord opened the door for her politely, but Jacques ignored her escape, now intent on spewing his poison at someone else. Lydia could see that the murderer had in some small way done her a favor by severing her relationship with Bulan before Jacques disappeared in a cloud of controversy.

Once outside, Lydia dialed a car service. She carried each box out on the curb and set it down on the snowy ground. She stomped her feet and blew on her hands to keep warm while she waited. She wanted to be far away from Bulan as soon as possible.

Chapter 15

It took two trips from the car service to get all her prints into her building. It was a sad end to her triumphant New York debut. The state of her building only deepened her foul mood. Her super was a lazy man normally, but lately he'd really been letting things slip in the building. She grimaced as she pushed the door open. The lock on the front door was broken again. The floors were sticky and dirty, and she had no idea when he'd swept the halls last. She set her boxes down in the hall.

The mailbox doors were standing open again, too. Anyone could have taken her checks, lifted her credit-card bill, or read her mail. She was furious. She was going to have to call the post office and complain again. She should program that number and one for the housing department on speed dial. The landlord kept shortening the hours they had heat, which was illegal in New York. He never did anything he was supposed to do unless he was constantly prodded.

Lydia took out her mail, catching it just before it fell onto the floor. She tried to wedge her mailbox door shut, but it just kept falling open again. She gave up after a few tries and looked through her mail. She paged through a few bills, the latest copy of *American Photographer* magazine, the promised cacti postcard from her parents, and a blank envelope. Blank envelopes didn't normally find their way through the postal system. She wondered if it had fallen out of the magazine.

Curious, Lydia opened the envelope. A photo fell out onto the floor next to a cigarette butt. She picked up the picture gingerly. The image was hauntingly familiar, like seeing a new interpretation of a famous work of art. This time the artwork was hers, and the scene was all too real. Jane Doe number five lay in a pile of trash in full garish color, her body twisted in agony from trying to expel the poison in her system. Lydia's stomach lurched.

As in the original photograph Lydia had taken, Jane Doe was wearing jeans and a red shirt, her hair was shaved, and she had a crude tattoo inked on her fingers. The light was not as delicate, and the camera had been placed closer to the model. The trash under her body had not been neatly arranged, and looked like it had been scattered by the body on top. Lydia had tried to imagine what it felt like to be poisoned by heroin when she had photographed Jenny as Jane Doe number five, and had arranged her limbs in a fashion that echoed classical paintings like *The Rape of Europa.* But as far as the photograph in her hand was concerned, no imagination was required. This time, it wasn't a staged performance for the camera. Jenny was really dead. The killer had struck again.

Lydia sank down onto the stairs, clutching her mail. Part of her had hoped and prayed that Marie's death was an isolated incident. Despite the attack on Jacques, she hoped the killer had retreated back into whatever hole he'd crawled out of. The photograph in her hands proved he was just getting started. And he knew where Lydia lived. She was terrified. She suddenly wanted to leave New York, home of psychopaths and murderers, and never look back.

She dug in her purse until she found Detective Romero's card and her phone. His cell number was neatly printed in the corner. She had forgotten that his first name was Daniel. She dialed the number with shaking hands.

Romero sounded tired and irritated when he finally answered his cell after seven rings. "You found a what?"

"A photograph in my mailbox of another victim. He knows where I live." Lydia tried to calm her breathing. She wished she'd paid more attention in that yoga class.

He cursed with great fluency, and Lydia held the phone slightly away from her ear until he was finished. "We'll be there in fifteen minutes. Don't touch anything." Romero hung up abruptly. Lydia stared at her cell phone angrily. She was getting tired of people hanging up on her.

She got shakily to her feet. She was having trouble comprehending the true depths of the problem at hand. A crazy killer, someone she probably knew, was out there somewhere. He knew where she lived, and probably where she worked, and could even be following her. He was basing his murders on her photographs and he wanted her to know it. He was getting closer and closer, and he had probably come into her building to leave the photograph of his latest victim in her mailbox.

She stared at her boxes for a moment before remembering that they even belonged to her. She had to get her prints upstairs. She went on autopilot and took each box upstairs and set it down outside her door. On the second trip, she fumbled for her keys and opened her door. The apartment looked just like she had left it that morning, but a horrifying thought occurred to her. Maybe the killer was inside her apartment. With her cell phone clutched in one hand, she made herself look under the bed and behind the shower curtain for an intruder. She checked behind her clothes, but the boogeyman didn't jump out. She was alone. She staggered back on trembling legs to the living room and sat down on the couch.

It felt like hours passed before Romero and Detective Wong finally arrived together. Lydia got up to let them in when she heard their impatient knock, and she pointed wordlessly to where she'd dropped the evidence on the table. The detectives advanced toward the photograph as they had approached her locker, pulling on latex gloves. Romero picked it up, and he and Wong examined it in silence. He picked up and studied the envelope next to it.

"This is the envelope it came in?" Lydia nodded. "How was it delivered?"

"My mailbox was open. Anyone who got inside the building could have put it in there."

"And the front door . . ."

"The lock is broken more than it works. We practically put out a welcome mat for thieves."

"We'll have to talk to the neighbors and see if they saw anyone suspicious," Romero said to Wong. Lydia winced. The last thing she needed was for all her neighbors to know she was involved in a murder investigation. Mrs. Zablonsky, an elderly Polish woman, would probably petition their landlord to have her kicked out for being a bad seed.

"Do you recognize the victim?" Wong asked, looking like she wished she could put the cuffs on Lydia without any more messing around. Lydia didn't blame her. The night before, she had found Jacques, and now this.

Lydia nodded, close to tears. "It's Jenny Powers. She's a painter in my critique group. She's posed like the body in my photograph of Jane Doe number five. The real one was a teenager—a runaway, they guessed—who died of an overdose—poisoned heroin. They found her body dumped in an alley."

"Which alley did you use?"

Lydia understood in a flash. The original location of the murder didn't matter. But it was important to know where Lydia had shot the photo. Somehow the killer knew where she'd taken the pictures. Her stomach churned again. The killer had to be someone she knew. But who? The only people who knew the details of her shoots were Emily, Georgia, and Marie. Could one of them have passed on the information to a killer?

She swallowed her nausea with difficulty. "There's a little alley off of Hope Street between Havemeyer and Roebling. I asked the landlord if I could use it, and he said he didn't mind, as long as I cleaned up afterward."

Romero flipped open his cell phone. He dialed and spoke brusquely to the person on the other end. He said, "I need a patrol car to go to Hope Street. Have them secure the area, but don't let them contaminate it. I'll be there in five."

Wong had already slipped the photograph into a plastic sleeve and was heading for the door like she couldn't get out of Lydia's apartment fast enough. Lydia remembered seeing a movie once where a woman killed people while she was sleepwalking and never remembered it when she woke up, and Lydia wondered if Wong had seen it, too. She couldn't even imagine having an unconscious wish to kill her models, though. They were her friends and they made her art projects possible.

Romero moved over to the couch, where Lydia was sitting. He crouched down in front of her and studied her face. She had never noticed the warmth of his brown eyes. His chin was covered with stubble and he looked like he hadn't slept in days. She realized he was trying hard to solve the case, and she felt grateful.

"Are you going to be okay here?"

"Here?" Lydia asked vaguely.

"The killer was inside your building today. You shouldn't stay here."

Lydia shook her head. The last thing she wanted to do was to leave home. Home was just about the only thing that felt secure to her right now. "I'm fine."

Romero studied her for a moment. "How about having a friend come over?"

Lydia thought for a moment about calling Georgia, but she knew that Georgia would be upset when she heard what had happened and would probably want to be comforted herself. She felt too tired to deal with someone else's emotions. "I'm fine. Honest. I'm just shaken up."

Romero continued to watch her like he was waiting for her to crack up. She shifted uncomfortably in her seat. He had never been so warm with her before. He must really think I'm in big trouble, she thought.

"It would be no problem for us to drop you at a friend's house on our way. This woman isn't going anywhere," he said grimly.

Lydia attempted to smile at his graveyard cop humor. "Right now, she needs you more than I do."

He was waiting for her to show she was all right. But Lydia wasn't sure if she was capable of acting normal right now. She felt as if she were underwater and trying not to drown. She needed to take a shower and try to clear her mind. Lydia struggled to get to her feet, forcing Romero to stand, as well.

She reached out to touch his arm but ended up clutching it like a lifeline when her legs didn't feel steady. "Do me a favor, will you?"

Romero nodded.

"Catch the guy who killed her."

Chapter 16

Back at the office the next day, Lydia tried to get back to normal and not jump every time the phone rang. She was avoiding looking at a paper and reading the sordid details of Jenny's death. But after the murders of both Marie and Jenny, her priority was keeping the rest of her models safe. If some lunatic had decided to knock off one by one everyone who had posed for her pictures, she felt obligated to do anything she could to stop him. She asked Emily, Georgia, and Ruby to meet her at Olé for an emergency meeting that evening. If they brainstormed together, maybe they could figure out who might be doing this terrible thing, and find a way to make sure it didn't happen again.

The D'Angelos had wrapped up the case of Mr. Carroll's cheating wife in record time. She needed to tally the receipts for an expense report, type up Frankie's notes, and send an invoice. She also needed to put captions on the photographs in case the divorce went through and they needed to present the evidence in court. Mr. Carroll had been right about his wife. She had been meeting a real estate agent regularly at a local cheap hotel with a neon sign that read AIR CONDITIONING. It was doubtful that they were discussing making an offer on a new property. Frankie had managed to snap a few good shots, but Lydia would have tried to give the photos a bit more atmosphere—perhaps a vacancy sign that had lost all its vowels, or plastic daffodils in window boxes.

She then moved onto Frankie's receipts, but it wasn't exactly action-packed stuff. She finally got to the end of a pile of strange scrawls, which she at last deciphered as gas station receipts. She entered them neatly into an Excel document and printed it out.

Lydia let herself savor the accomplishment for another five seconds before she opened up the billing file. She had to pay the office bills that had been piling up. A bookkeeper checked her work, but it was her responsibility to enter all the check amounts into the computer. Mathematics was not her specialty, so she was always afraid she would make a mistake. She made herself concentrate totally on the task.

An hour later, Frankie swaggered into the office. Lydia opened her mouth to greet him and was startled to see Frankie's companion, an attractive blond woman. The woman was his height, thin but busty, and her look was a mix of gangster moll and New York sophisticate. Her charcoal turtleneck and tweed pants were designer items and pricey, but she wore far too much makeup.

"Leo, Lydia—this is Heather Pruitt." Frankie's face flushed with pride as he threw his arm around Heather's shoulders, and Heather gave them a tight smile with her bright red lips as she looked around the office.

"Pleased to meet you, Heather," Leo said stiffly.

Lydia waved weakly from her desk. "Nice to meet you, too." Lydia wasn't sure what she'd expected Frankie's girlfriend to look like, but it wasn't this. She'd honestly expected a younger version of Mama.

"Oh, sweetie pie, it's just like you described," Heather gushed as she clutched Frankie's arm with long red fake nails that looked like claws. Lydia stared at her desktop to avoid looking at Leo. Frankie must have met Heather awhile ago in order to be on cutesy nickname terms with her already.

"It's not a big business, but Leo and I are proud of it," Frankie told her. He sucked in his gut and beamed from ear to ear.

Heather fluttered her eyelashes at Leo. "I can't imagine being a private eye. It must be so dangerous." It wasn't, particularly when guys like Frankie sat in the office and read the paper, but Lydia wasn't going to say anything.

Leo cleared his throat. "It has its moments."

There was a short, uncomfortable silence. Lydia felt bad for Frankie. He probably thought this woman was the best thing since pop-tops, and they were treating her like warmed-over lentil loaf. She decided to do what she could to help out.

"How did you two meet?" Couples in love always liked to talk about how they first got together.

Frankie blushed so hard, even his hands turned fuchsia. Lydia hadn't known that he could turn that shade, and she had to stop herself from staring at him.

"Don't be embarrassed, honey pot." Heather pinched Frankie's florid cheek. "We met on GotAnything. I just knew from his first e-mail that he was someone special. I'm so happy to be meeting his family today." Lydia almost blushed herself. She hadn't meant to embarrass him.

Soon after, Frankie led Heather away for a romantic lunch at

Mama D'Angelo's restaurant, an experience she didn't envy either of them having. Frankie was delusional if he thought his mother was going to like this woman. Heather was anything but the traditional Italian-American girl of Mama's dreams. She doubted Heather was even interested in cooking. And Heather was crazy to agree to meet his mother so soon. Frankie adored his mother, and listened to her opinions. But it wasn't Lydia's life or her fault if they became the next Romeo and Juliet.

Olé was a small Mexican restaurant and bar on the main drag. During the summer, it provided great people-watching opportunities. The location was also close and convenient for everyone. The food was best avoided entirely, except for the nachos, but the drinks were always good. Sitting down on a padded stool at the dark wood bar, Lydia ordered the biggest margarita they had. She desperately needed something strong in order to talk this through with her models Georgia, Emily, and Ruby. Ruby was an amazing contortionist and she had posed for quite a few of Lydia's photographs that had required unusual or strenuous poses.

The place was nearly empty because of the early hour. The filthy floor and scarred wooden bar looked dingy and sad without a crowd. Luckily, Georgia arrived before too long. They kissed cheeks and admired each other's accessories. Georgia had some pretty earrings that looked like butterflies, and a new bracelet with a chunk of amber embedded in the gold.

"Did you hear that Bad Enemies has broken up?" Georgia asked, referring to her old band.

"They couldn't go on without you," Lydia teased, munching on blue nacho chips from the bowl on the bar. "What's Brian going to do?"

"He's good enough to play drums for anyone," Georgia said carelessly. Brian had had a crush on her for years, and she just treated him like a little brother, much to his dismay. He was unmistakably too nice and did not have the dangerous edge that attracted Georgia.

They gossiped for a few minutes about people they'd seen lately who'd made unfortunate choices of haircuts or hair color. There had been so much tragedy in the last week, and they both felt emotionally exhausted. Later, they would talk again about Jenny and Marie and death, but right now they needed to reside in the land of the living.

Georgia Rae reached out and examined a lock of Lydia's hair. "You should come by the salon for a new cut. Yours is looking a bit worn down these days."

"I wish I could find the time." She looked down at her velour tunic, black skirt, and boots and thought everything about her felt tired. She desperately needed a beauty treatment and some new clothes.

The bartender delivered a strawberry daiquiri into Georgia's hands. "Yum, yum." They clinked glasses.

"To us." Despite ups and downs, and a variety of boyfriends, Georgia and Lydia had remained best friends for years longer than many people stayed married. Moments like these reminded Lydia of how lucky she was to have a friend like Georgia. The events of the past week had just reinforced how precious her friends were to her.

They both sipped their drinks and looked around the bar. Olé was starting to fill up, and they were going to have a hard time reserving bar stools for Emily and Ruby.

"Emily isn't usually late," Lydia fretted. She checked her watch. She hated to act so paranoid, but it was hard not to worry with a killer out there preying on her friends.

"It's okay. She'll be here."

Lydia checked her cell phone for the tenth time. Suddenly, an announcement popped up on her screen that she had a message. "I hate how your phone doesn't ring and then all of a sudden it tells you that you have a message." She checked her voice mail. It was Ruby. She sounded shaky and upset.

"I can't take this right now. First Marie, then Jenny. I'm going home to Connecticut until this whole thing calms down," Ruby said. Lydia saved the message and shut her phone. She placed it carefully on the bar and stared at it for a moment.

Georgia watched her. "What's going on?"

Lydia filled her in. "Maybe Ruby has the right idea about fleeing Williamsburg. It's not safe."

Georgia was finally ready to get down to the nitty-gritty. "Lydia, you should really consider that you might be the target. Someone jealous of your talent is ruining your art for you." Georgia patted her lips carefully with a napkin. "After that terrible experience I had with the stalker last summer, I can tell you this kind of thing is no joke. I was a mess for months afterward. And my stalker didn't succeed in hurting me, except emotionally."

"I'm not going to run away. Although if you want to go on an extended vacation, I won't complain. . . ."

Georgia shook her head firmly. "I'm not running, either. Surely there are other ways to stay safe and catch this crazy guy."

"How about the buddy system?" Teachers used it in school, so they must have found it worked.

"That might not be a bad idea. Each one of us would be responsible for someone else."

"We could call one another regularly, and if we don't hear back, we call the cops." Lydia thought she'd heard someone had to be missing for twenty-four hours, but maybe Romero would listen to her if she sounded the alarm.

Georgia lectured Lydia about the poor security in her apartment building until Emily arrived at last, windblown and red-faced from the cold.

"Oh my God!" Emily wailed. "You've got to help me!"

Lydia set down her drink hard, splashing it on the counter, and leaped off her bar stool. Georgia wasn't far behind. They scanned behind Emily for pursuers as they rushed toward her, but she was alone.

"What happened? Are you okay?" Lydia asked, examining Emily for visible wounds.

Emily staggered to the bar and sat down. "They've called Stuart in for questioning!"

Lydia's shoulders slumped with relief. This was a crisis she could handle. "They're questioning everyone who knew Marie. They're just trying to find her killer."

"But I'm sure they suspect Stuart of killing her."

Lydia returned to the bar and took a large restorative swallow of her drink. Why would the cops think Stuart would have any reason to kill Marie? As far as she knew, they were friends. He was shy and a bit bumbling when it came to dating, but she'd seen no signs of a cold-blooded killer in his personality or actions in the years that she'd known him.

"Have they found some evidence that points to Stuart?"

Emily shook her head and looked away. She evidently knew something. "We can't help you if you don't tell us what's going on, Emily."

"Stuart and Marie dated about a year ago."

"What!" Lydia was shocked. She'd always figured everyone knew that Emily was in love with Stuart and so they'd kept their hands off.

Georgia smiled smugly. "I suspected there was a bit of sexual tension, but they kept it very hush-hush."

Lydia frowned at Georgia, annoyed. She hated when people disclosed their hunches after the fact. It absolutely did not count. "Dating someone is no reason to arrest anyone. I wouldn't worry about it."

Emily played with her purse strap. "They also found out that he and Marie had a big fight right before she died."

Lydia frowned. She was feeling completely out of it. "About what?"

"What does it matter? He didn't kill her. We have to do something."

Lydia thought it would be a shame for him to go to prison before he and Emily even got a chance to go out on a date, but she wasn't sure what they could do about it.

"What he needs right now is a good lawyer."

"I called Volunteer Lawyers for the Arts. I had to pull a lot of strings, but they've agreed to help." Emily was always at her best when she had a long "To do" list.

Lydia knew that her fellow photographers had used Volunteer Lawyers for the Arts to set up small-business status with the IRS and help them with contracts, but she'd never heard of the organization helping out with a murder defense before. She supposed it was better than having no lawyer at all.

"You have some friends in law enforcement, don't you?" Emily wheedled. "I mean, you work for private eyes."

"They don't do homicide cases," Lydia said. The D'Angelos would be horrified if she brought it up. They also did not do pro bono work.

"You're our best hope," Emily implored. "None of the other artists knows anyone who can help."

Lydia didn't want to promise anything. Romero would probably tell her to go play with flammable objects if she tried to find out what he had on Stuart. But she was curious to know where the case was headed. Lydia could imagine calling Marie, if she were still alive, to find out what dirt she knew about Stuart and what they had fought about. Sadly, that option was not available.

"I'll talk to Detective Romero, but I doubt he'll tell me anything," Lydia warned Emily. "Now let's talk about our safety. There's a killer still at large. Georgia and I have a couple of ideas."

The friends made a pact to check in with one another regularly, take taxis after dark, double-bolt their doors, and not take candy from strangers. Lydia wasn't sure what else they could do to stay safe, and she prayed that what they were doing would be enough.

Chapter 17

"You can't bring that woman on a stakeout with you. She's not a trained detective," Leo hissed.

"Heather really wants to learn. She's very observant." Frankie sounded hurt.

"Heather is—" Leo broke off, not able even to say what Heather was in his eyes.

Lydia had dragged herself into the office that morning, clutching a large cappuccino as if it were a life raft, and now she was hiding out behind her computer, trying to pretend she wasn't listening to the D'Angelos fight about Heather. She knew she looked like she'd hardly slept, because she hadn't. She'd tossed and turned all night, dreaming about Jenny and Marie. The dreams had been horrible and vividly real. She'd had to watch her friends die while she was frozen and unable to move or help.

The only possible costume that morning had been her Wild

West outfit, a ruffled denim skirt, red leather cowboy boots, and a tight red T-shirt that spelled out "Cowgirl" in rhinestones. If she'd had a fake six-shooter, she would have put it in her holster, but instead she'd tied a red bandanna around her neck and declared herself ready to duke it out with the bad guys.

Leo finally noticed that he and Frankie weren't alone. "Lydia, could you take some petty cash and get us some more stamps? We're almost out."

Lydia knew they still had an adequate supply in the drawer, but she took the excuse to make her escape. The sun was out as Lydia left the office. The snow had melted and the day was slowly warming up, and she thought she might have spotted a tiny green leaf trying to push its way through the soil next to one of the small anemic trees in the middle of the sidewalk. She wished it luck. It was true what T. S. Eliot had said about spring being cruel. Life lately had been filled with death, and in the end that's what made it life. She turned her face to the sun and let its warmth wash over her. A cool wind rushed into her ears, but at least her nose was warm.

Lydia strolled along Leonard Street, wondering if she had time to stop in at a vintage store on her way back. She decided that the D'Angelos wanted to work out their differences without her, so she had carte blanche. She was glad when she stopped in at the Spotted Cat, because they had a pair of purple suede boots that were exactly her size. She deserved a treat after all her trauma the past week, so she indulged.

She made her way back to the office, feeling lighter and happier than she had for days. But at the entrance, she stopped and gaped. Frankie's girlfriend, Heather, sat at Lydia's desk, going through Lydia's drawers as if she already owned the joint. She was wearing a microscopic black leather miniskirt and a fuchsia turtleneck sweater. She looked up and gave Lydia a smug smile.

"Your outfit is so . . . entertaining," Heather said.

Lydia gave her a fake smile in return. "I know *Vogue* advises people to stay out of miniskirts after thirty, but you wear it well."

Heather was probably afraid if she frowned, she would get permanent wrinkles around her eyes, so she allowed herself only to narrow her eyes at Lydia. "I hope you don't mind, but Frankie said it would be all right for me to sit here today."

Lydia really hated when anyone touched her stuff, especially people who looked like they couldn't be trusted. She gave an unintelligible reply, then shot Frankie a look that promised to tell all and then some to Mama D'Angelo. Mama had been right to fear Frankie's dating spree. This woman was bad news. Frankie wisely ducked behind his newspaper. Leo was nowhere in sight.

Lydia plopped down in the guest chair and dropped her bag on the floor. "All right. I'll just sit over here and drink my coffee, then." She put her cowboys boots up on an unoccupied chair. This was war. No desk, no work. If the D'Angelos didn't like it, they could just scrape Heather's behind off Lydia's desk chair.

Frankie lowered his paper to give Heather a pleading gaze. He didn't have the guts to say anything, but he knew that Leo would have no such scruples when he came back. Heather allowed herself a very tiny and brief frown. If Lydia wasn't going to go head-to-head with her over the desk, but instead allowed the D'Angelos to do her fighting for her, then needling her was clearly no fun. Heather stood up slowly and gave a little fake yawn to indicate that she was bored by the exchange.

"I know how busy you are, so let me just move over here so you can get started." Heather pulled up another chair alongside the desk chair and perched on it. "I hope you won't mind if I look over your shoulder today. I'm so curious about how Frankie's business works."

"Would that be okay, Lydia?" Frankie asked anxiously. "I told Heather you wouldn't mind." Lydia would have preferred to go to the dentist for a root canal, but she doubted Heather would appreciate her sarcasm.

"Oh, sure," Lydia said casually, deciding to put Heather to work doing mind-numbing tasks until she ran out screaming. Frankie had brought a barracuda into their midst. Heather was after not only Frankie's money but Lydia's job, as well. The job might be dull, but right now it was paying Lydia's large stack of bills. "We just got in some phone records from a corporate client. You can help me if you want."

Heather tried to smile enthusiastically, but it was obvious she was allergic to real work. Lydia gave her a few Hi-Liters and told her what to look for. They were searching for strange numbers that might indicate an employee was using the work line to make expensive and unauthorized calls. Lydia started on another page, watching out of the corner of her eye as Heather fiddled with the highlighting pens. Heather chewed on the end of one delicately, staining it with her lipstick, but didn't manage to mark any numbers as suspicious.

Fifteen minutes later, Lydia was not surprised to see Heather get up to go snuggle up to Frankie and discuss newspaper headlines with him. Lydia smiled, and finally allowed herself to work on balancing their checkbook. The phone rang and Lydia grabbed it before Frankie could.

"D'Angelo Investigations, Lydia speaking."

"Lydia," Mama D'Angelo boomed. "Is she there?"

It was pointless to pretend that she didn't understand whom Mama was referring to. "Yes."

Mama breathed heavily into the receiver. "We're in big trouble. Frankie thinks he's in love. He's already talking about rings!"

"Have you talked to Leo about the problem?" Lydia asked, shooting a glance in the couple's direction. They seemed oblivious to the call and Mama D'Angelo's distress.

"He thinks it will pass. I am not so sure."

Lydia doubted it herself. Heather was pretty determined, and Frankie wasn't exactly inundated with other offers. Lydia's cell phone started tweeting from under her desk. "I'll have to talk to you about the problem at another time," she told Mama. Lydia searched in her bag and all over her desk before she finally found the phone behind a three-hole punch. She examined the incoming number. The screen unhelpfully read UNKNOWN. Corporate clients occasionally showed up that way, so she had no choice but to answer it.

"Hello, this is Lydia," she said smoothly.

"This is Ron Jamison from the *New York Observer.*" His gravelly voice sounded like he smoked at least a pack a day of unfiltered cigarettes. Lydia had sent out over a hundred press releases for her gallery opening but had heard back from only one local paper. She allowed herself to feel a tiny thrill that a big paper like the *Observer* might be interested in her show.

"An anonymous source told us that you took some pretty graphic pictures, and now a killer is on a rampage in Williamsburg, really murdering people just like the ones in your photos."

Lydia sat in shocked silence. Her heart beat loudly in her ears. She couldn't breathe. Someone had leaked the story to the papers. Everyone was going to find out about the killer using her pictures as his blueprints for murder. The police were going to think she was the one who'd leaked the story, but the last thing she wanted was for the newspapers to start discussing her art and its relationship to the murders.

Who could have leaked the story? The cops? They'd told her leaking it would jeopardize their investigation, and she did not doubt that solving the crime would give them much more positive publicity than having their investigation compromised. But the only other possible source for the leak that she could think of was the murderer. And Lydia could think of only one reason for him to leak it: to incriminate her further.

Lydia had to bring herself back down to earth to understand what Ron Jamison was saying next. "We were wondering what your price would be to sell us your originals for our story."

A week ago, she hadn't been able to move a single print off the gallery wall. Too bad the newspaper's motives were so bad and she had to say "No, thank you" to her first big break in years. "No one was murdered in my photographs. My pictures are murder recreations using live models."

"Yeah, sure." Jamison sounded bored, like he was flipping through papers on his desk looking for his next splashy story. "But we heard someone is killing your models and posing them just like in your pictures. We were hoping to print yours to give our readers a sense of the tragedy unfolding."

Jamison wasn't concerned with Jenny or Marie, just in selling papers. She wondered if she could keep him on the phone long enough to extract a little information of her own.

"Where did you get your information about my photographs?"

"I wish I could say, but my source is protected, Miss McKenzie."

Lydia's grip tightened on her cell phone. She didn't want her photographs to be used to exploit the pain and suffering of her friends. She had been unable to prevent their deaths, but at least she could stop the paper from hurting their families even more. "My photographs are not for sale. Marie LaFarge and Jenny Powers were friends, and I would do nothing to harm the investigation of their murders."

Chapter 18

The sun and warmth of the day before had vanished, leaving the day of Marie's memorial service cold and gray. The low dark clouds fit exactly with Lydia's mood. As she strolled over to the memorial service, she thought about how Marie would have loved to arrange her own service. She would probably have found a troupe of acrobats, a sultan's tent, and bagpipers. The party would have been unique, exciting, and as fabulous as Marie.

Lydia stood at the door of the Bank and looked around. The waterfall and pool of water built at the center of the loft space were lighted up and looked magical at night, but during the day they looked stark and strange. The room where the service was being held was still empty of people. Emily was flitting around arranging chairs. She still had on her pink coat and looked like a tiny frantic butterfly.

Lydia shed her own coat, revealing a simple dark blue dress with a scoop neck and high waist. Her outfit was saved from looking like something a schoolgirl would wear by black stiletto knee-high boots. She put her coat down on a folding chair and waylaid Emily. "Can I help?"

Emily gave Lydia a big hug and looked relieved to see her. "I'm still in shock. First Marie and then Jenny. She was supposed to open the service and talk about Marie today."

"I knew they were friends, but I didn't know they were really close," Lydia said as she helped Emily move the lectern.

"They were roommates when they first came to New York, so they'd known each other forever."

This was news to Lydia. She assumed they'd known each other through the critique group and had occasionally hung out. She wondered how much they'd had in common, and if perhaps they'd shared an acquaintance who'd had it in for them both. Her mind buzzed with possibilities.

"Are you sure Jeanne Goldberg from *Beauty* is going to show?" Emily asked uncertainly. "She's an awfully busy woman. . . ."

"Oh, she'll show, don't worry. Marie was very special to her," Lydia said, reassuring her. She didn't add that she possessed something Jeanne desperately wanted. She had told no one about her discovery.

Emily looked around the room anxiously. "The wall in front looks totally bare, doesn't it? Could you get some of the flower baskets by the door and put them up here? I have to find a microphone somewhere that works."

Lydia went to find the flowers. Although she had enjoyed setting the scene for her murder photographs, flower arranging was foreign to her. She grabbed a couple of large baskets, carried them to the wall behind the lectern, and set them down. They looked a little lonely, so she went to grab some more. Luckily, Georgia wandered in a few minutes later.

"Can you help me take some of these flowers up front? Emily asked me to do some decorating."

Flower arranging was probably inscribed in all good southern girls' DNA, so Lydia knew she'd picked the right person. Georgia saw the space they were decorating and shook her head.

"Rustle me up a small table, sugar. We need flowers on different levels to really enhance the space."

Lydia hurried off to locate a table. She was glad to be following orders. Thinking creatively about flowers, her speech, and murder suspects threatened to send her brain into overload. She found a small fold-up stand against a wall and took it over to Georgia.

Friends and relations began to flow into the room. Emily made sure that everyone got a chance to give their condolences to Marie's mom at the front and sign a memory book. Marie's mother was already on her second box of tissues, and the service had not even started yet. Lydia's heart went out to her. She still couldn't believe that Marie was really gone. Lydia spotted Stuart and Rain as each of them came in, but she decided to wait until later to talk to them. She wanted to keep her eye out for Jeanne Goldberg.

A few minutes before the ceremony was due to start, Jeanne swept in, looking aggressively chic in a black wool suit. Lydia admired her style, if not her manners. She walked over to Jeanne.

"Do you have it?" Jeanne was as blunt as always. She probably preferred to call it "direct."

Lydia reached into her pocket and took out an envelope containing the photograph of Jeanne kissing another woman. Jeanne stared at the envelope, as if she were eager to snatch it and make a run for it. "Of course. But I'll hand it over only on the condition that you say only nice things about Marie during the service. I want her family to have only good memories of her, understood?" Lydia made sure to keep her voice low so that no one else would hear.

Jeanne nodded. "She was a good photographer."

"Great." Lydia handed over the envelope. Jeanne peeked inside just to make sure the photo was there.

"And the negatives?"

"Already destroyed," Lydia said, lying. She did not have any idea where they were, but she was pretty confident that Marie's family would throw them away if they ever found them. They definitely weren't the type to blackmail anyone. She was positive that Jeanne was mistaken about Marie's intentions, too.

"Thank you," Jeanne said, still looking a little uncertain. She probably expected Lydia to demand money and favors for the photograph. They stood together for a few seconds, looking awkward.

"I hope someday your workplace will be somewhere where you won't be embarrassed to introduce the love of your life to your coworkers," Lydia said, feeling a little preachy. Jeanne only tossed her skunklike hair and strode away. Lydia wasn't sure if she was in denial or just buried deep in an impossibly large walk-in closet. Either way, she felt sorry for Jeanne.

When the chairs were filled with Marie's family, friends, and coworkers, Emily signaled to Georgia. Georgia walked up to the lectern's microphone, now placed in front of a lovely arrangement of lilies and mums. She was wearing an elegant black dress, and three-inch heels, and she had tucked a muted yellow flower behind one ear.

Georgia began to sing "Amazing Grace" a cappella. The song had probably been sung a million times at funerals, but Georgia's rendition made the hair at the back of Lydia's neck stand on end. Her voice was marvelous, and she was putting all of her love for

Marie into the song. Lydia sniffed into a tissue and hoped that she wasn't going to lose it when it was her turn to speak.

As the last note died away, the room was quiet except for the hum of the heater. Emily dashed up and embraced Georgia. "We are here today to honor the memory of our friend Marie LaFarge. We will miss her terribly," Emily said, then called up a member of Marie's family to speak.

Marie's father marched stiffly to the microphone. He was a stocky man, stuffed into a suit that had probably fit him better twenty years ago. He was choked up, but he managed to convey the true feeling of loss for the family. Marie was their shining star. She'd come to New York and created a life that they did not quite understand, but they were proud of all her accomplishments anyway. Marie's mother sobbed loudly in the front row, too overcome to speak.

Emily called on Jeanne Goldberg next. Lydia noticed for the first time that Jeanne's suit skirt was extremely short. She had the legs to carry it off, but it just didn't look appropriate for a memorial. Lydia held her breath and waited to hear what she would say.

"Marie worked for me for three years at *Beauty.* She had a natural gift for fashion, and she was always on the cutting edge with her innovative ideas. She also made everyone—the talent, the assistants, everyone—comfortable with her warmth and kindness." Jeanne made Marie sound like a saint, which was what Lydia had instructed her to do. But Marie had been no saint. Saints, Lydia was sure, didn't throw wild parties, or have reckless affairs. Marie was interesting because she had always been a well-rounded, vibrant person, with all a normal person's faults and weaknesses.

Jeanne marched back to her seat, and Lydia was glad she did not just take off after having fulfilled her promise. Emily called on Pip

Ensler, and he got up and shuffled to the microphone. He was dressed in some sort of navy blue baggy suit that looked like it belonged to someone much taller and fatter, and he had a white T-shirt underneath. She couldn't believe that Marie had found him attractive, and she still didn't know what Marie had seen in his work.

"Marie always believed in me and thought that my paintings really spoke to her. When I was feeling low, she commissioned a piece from me and helped me keep going." His sentiments were nice, but he was talking more about himself than Marie. The speech was typical Pip. She let her mind wander as he continued to mumble into the microphone. The next thing she knew, Emily called her name. She took a deep breath and walked up to the front of the room. The audience looked much larger from the podium.

"I wanted to find something to read that was special to Marie, but in the end I didn't find anything that really fit her." Lydia cleared her throat. "The truth is that words were never as important to Marie as images, and she could set a scene better than anyone I ever met. If anyone got in the way of her vision, though, she could also throw a humdinger of a temper tantrum." Everyone in the the crowd laughed a little through their tears. "But she was warm and generous, and she loved to bring people together. I met the most amazing people at her house, and had some of the best evenings of my life there."

Lydia told a simple story about meeting Marie at the darkroom and bonding over black licorice and clothes. They became instant friends, and Marie had always been willing to drop everything and go out on an adventure. "She was my friend, and I miss her very much," Lydia concluded, and walked back to her seat. She allowed the tears to flow then, knowing that she had a pack of tissues in her bag.

Georgia Rae got up and gave Lydia a quick squeeze in passing.

Her eyes were red and a good deal of her makeup had been wiped off. She went to the microphone and sang "Many Rivers to Cross." At first, her singing was shaky, and then her voice began to soar. Anyone who had managed to keep from crying earlier pretty much lost it then.

Emily was already setting out food at the back of the room when Georgia sang the last note. She had run the service with frightening efficiency. If she hadn't also been a great portrait photographer, Lydia would have recommended that she start an event-planning business. She was a natural.

Lydia strolled back to snag some fresh fruit and Brie before the hungry hordes descended on the food table. Emily was laying out crackers in neat rows and biting gloss off her lip.

"Emily, that was great. You did a fantastic job."

Emily did not even pause as she continued to fill the platter with crackers. "Thanks."

Lydia munched for a few seconds. "I was wondering something. How well did Stuart know Jenny?"

"Stuart had nothing to do with Jenny," Emily hissed, grabbing a container of toothpicks.

"The police have to have something on Stuart besides his dating Marie and fighting with her once." Lydia was getting a little tired of being asked for help and then not having any information.

Emily began poking lots of toothpicks around the base of a giant pineapple centerpiece so it would stay upright and quit falling into the crackers. She was putting in so many that the pineapple was beginning to look as if it had been attacked by thousands of tiny archers. "He knew Jacques, too."

"Ah," Lydia said. To know Jacques was to dislike him, so probably Stuart had argued with Jacques, too.

"Jacques accused Stuart of stealing from him when he sold a piece that he showed in the gallery to someone who saw it before the show." This was a sticky area, one that confused many artists. The truth was that the art world was based on relationships. If you got the reputation for being greedy and unscrupulous, galleries became uninterested in doing business with you.

"I hope Stuart didn't threaten to kill him or something." Emily stared at Lydia, alarmed, and Lydia groaned. Stuart had probably yelled something threatening to Jacques in front of witnesses. Lydia found it difficult to help someone who was so determined to screw up his own life. "The cops should know that not everyone does what they say in anger."

"I need to get some more crackers. There aren't nearly enough out," Emily said. She was distracted by the arrangements, and they were going to have to talk more later.

"Okay," Lydia said, spearing a strawberry with her fork and popping it into her mouth. It was the wrong season for the fruit, so it did not taste like much. She turned and eyed the crowd, spotting Romero across the room. He was leaning against the wall, watching her. He wore a well-tailored dark suit and looked too handsome for his own good.

Lydia started to move toward him through the crowd, but she kept running into people she knew who wanted to compliment her on her words at the service. But when she got to him, she realized she didn't know what she wanted to say. She felt like a girl angling for the first dance at the prom.

"Did you know that writer lives around the corner from you?"

Lydia was mystified. "What writer?"

"The one who wrote *Lost Girls.* Diana Gryziec. But she goes by Diana Randolph now."

"She lives in my neighborhood?" Lydia had never tried to look for the writer of the book. It made sense that Diana Gryziec lived in Williamsburg, since she had written about it, but Lydia'd never thought to search for her there.

Romero scanned the room behind her, his eyes coolly evaluating all the people at the memorial service.

"You think the murderer is going to stand up and confess or something?"

Romero shrugged, turning his gaze back to Lydia. "Have you considered the fact that you might have someone out to get you?"

Lydia grimaced. She'd had occasional arguments with people, but she'd never had anyone hate her before. She'd always tried her best not to hurt anyone else too badly. She couldn't imagine ever hating anyone enough to kill them. The person doing these murders must have a twisted soul to destroy wonderful, loving people like Jenny and Marie, especially if it's just to get even with me, Lydia thought.

"Think carefully. It could go back a long way."

Lydia had a horrible thought. "Do you think the guy who killed the original women, the ones I re-created in the photographs, could have killed Marie and Jenny, too?" Lydia's mind boggled. She had never felt so close to evil before. The murderer had to be some kind of soulless monster to have killed so many people.

Romero didn't even blink. "We're looking at all the possibilities. I hope you're being careful. I don't need more cases to keep me busy."

"I didn't know you cared, Romero," she said. He raised an eyebrow at her, so she continued quickly. "Don't worry about me; I'm taking a self-defense class. We're learning how to gouge people's eyes out."

Romero winced. “I got Marie’s calendar in the mail. It was very . . . illuminating.”

Lydia wondered how he had guessed it was from her. Perhaps they’d dusted it for fingerprints. He stood there, quietly watching her. She felt awkward and strange with him, as if something had just shifted and she didn’t know what to make of him or their conversation. Suddenly, she remembered her promise to Emily to inquire about Stuart.

“Is Stuart a suspect in the case?” she asked.

“I can’t discuss it.”

“But you did call him in for questioning,” she said, persistent. “He’s a gentle guy and wouldn’t hurt a fly.”

Romero pushed away from the wall and signaled across the room to someone. Lydia followed his eyes and saw Wong watching them both.

“Very few people are as they appear,” Romero told her. “You should stick to looking after yourself while I look for the murderer.”

Chapter 19

The second self-defense class was held late on a Sunday afternoon, just after the last service of the day at the church. They filed in just as the members of the congregation left to enjoy their Sunday dinner. Lydia could see right away that the second class was going to be a lot more serious than the first one. Instead of pretending to break kneecaps, they discussed weapons an attacker might use.

"Some women think that if they carry a gun, they'll be safer. Or a sharp object. Or Mace. But if your attacker is stronger than you are, chances are he can take it away from you and use it against you." Martina waited for her words to sink in. The women all shifted uncomfortably on their mats. The topic was particularly hard to digest in the cozy confines of the church basement, sitting amid the Christmas and Easter decorations from the previous year.

"Quite a few attackers will already have a weapon that they will attempt to use against the victim. It's important for you to be aware of this. Observe the situation before you act. Wait for your opportunity. Your goal is always to escape alive."

Martina showed them a few techniques to disarm an attacker by hitting a vulnerable part of the person's arm, but Lydia could tell that the rest of the group was as freaked-out as she was about the idea of a guy holding a gun or a knife on them. They all got up to try out the techniques, but everyone was just going through the motions.

"Your best line of defense is a surprising offense. Wait for your opportunity. Strike quickly. Grab the barrel of the gun and twist it away from you and out of his grasp. If it goes off, it won't be pointed at you."

Martina led them through more exercises with props, and they grabbed the green barrels of squirt guns and twisted them away. The action was easy in theory, but what if the person holding the gun wanted to kill you?

Lydia kept thinking about Marie and Jenny. The class forced her to imagine their last moments for the first time outside of her dreams. Was there a moment when they could have fought off the killer and escaped? If their attacker was someone they knew, they might have been lulled into a false sense of security before the killer struck. The scenario was both disturbing and likely.

Sensing the scattered energy in the room, Martina brought them together in a circle again. "Another dangerous situation we need to discuss is one that occurs with multiple attackers. Let's practice a scenario where you and a friend are walking together and three people attempt to attack you." Martina gestured to Lydia and Georgia to stand up. Out of a roomful of actors, Lydia grumbled to herself, Martina just had to pick me. Lydia had never been comfortable in front of a crowd, and she felt self-conscious performing the exercise. Luckily, she had on loose gaucho pants and a man's white dress shirt tied at the waist, so there was no danger of her ripping her clothes. Martina then picked three women who were always competing for center stage as the attackers.

"The first thing they're going to do to you is try to separate you. Why? Because one alone is more vulnerable. The two of you are strong together. What is the best way to be stronger still?" Martina looked into Lydia's eyes, and Lydia desperately wished she had an answer to her question. Martina was the kind of person Lydia really wanted to impress.

Martina gently tugged Lydia, so that she was standing back-to-back with Georgia, instead of next to her. "Now you have eyes and weapons in the back of your head. You can be twice as powerful. What do you do first?"

"Kick them in the kneecaps?" Lydia asked hopefully.

Martina shook her head.

"Yell as loud as you can," another student piped up from the back.

Right. Lydia knew that. Her desire to be the teacher's pet was interfering with her memory and cognitive powers. For the next half hour, Martina led them slowly through some techniques for getting away from their attackers, and Georgia and Lydia were forced to summon up whatever acting skills they had to pretend that the other women were menacing muggers instead of lovely actresses.

By the end of class, Lydia felt completely drained. Being in danger and constantly escaping had proved exhausting. She wanted the danger threatening her models to be over. Nothing she'd found in Marie's life pointed to a killer, and she wondered if there were any clues in Jenny's loft. She decided to swing by there on her way home and see if Jenny's roommates had seen anything or anyone suspicious. At least she wouldn't feel so paralyzed and reliant on the buddy system if she could get more information.

Lydia hopped on her bike and cycled up Metropolitan Avenue, doing her best to avoid homicidal garbage trucks and potholes big enough to hold a refrigerator as she made her way to Bushwick Avenue. Jenny's loft building was located about four blocks from her darkroom, so she knew the area well. She cycled the wrong way on one-way streets, up onto the sidewalk when something was in her way, and through red lights when there was no oncoming traffic. Lydia loved being a bicyclist because it meant never having to follow any inconvenient traffic rules. She missed her bike in the winter, when it was too cold and slippery to ride. Today, the weather was still cold, but the snow had melted, and she couldn't resist the freedom of having her own wheels.

She didn't see a good place to lock up her bike, so she pushed it up to the building entrance of 52 Meserole. She was reading the list of names on the buzzers and had just found the name Powers in 2B when a skateboarder who looked about thirteen burst out of the door. She held out her arm to stop the door from shutting. The skater threw down his board, which was covered with Japanese anime paintings, and leaped on top of it. He was lanky and ungraceful, but somehow he managed to stay on as he took off down the road.

The staircase was dark and dirty, with enormous dust bunnies on the steps, as well as an impressive collection of smashed beer cans and cigarette butts. Someone living there evidently loved to party. She locked her bike to the railing at the bottom of the stairs and hiked up to the second floor.

The door at the top of the stairs was propped open, so Lydia pushed her way in. The entrances to the lofts were off a long hallway. The landlord hadn't bothered to paint the wallboard or finish the rough wooden floor. Someone had used black gaffer's tape to write the numbers on the gray metal doors to the individual spaces. At 2B, she stopped and listened. Music played loudly from inside. She knocked. There was no answer, so she knocked again as loudly as she could.

A guy with no shirt on opened the door. His chest and arms were decorated with an enormous tattoo mural. She winced and tried to look anywhere but his skin. She hated tattoos. They always made her think of pain. Despite her work with death in her photos, she was not a big fan of pain. But his tattoo was difficult to ignore. It was some sort of tribute to Egypt, with pyramids jutting above his nipples, a cat lounging around his belly button, and gods prancing down his arms.

"I just found out about Jenny," Lydia told him truthfully, "so I had to come over."

The guy shook his head sadly, obviously assuming she had been a friend. "Doesn't it suck? She was my roomie, and I just can't believe it."

"Can I come in?" Lydia asked. "My name is Lydia."

The guy shrugged. "I'm Phoenix." Lydia followed him into the loft, wondering if the name had inspired the giant bird tattoo on his back, or the other way around.

The loft had a giant center room surrounded by four tiny cubiclelike rooms built from scrap drywall. "Do you think I could look around? I thought it might help me feel closer to her."

Phoenix shrugged again. "Her room is over there." Lydia wondered if the killer could have entered as easily as she just had. Phoenix was remarkably trusting.

Lydia ducked her head to enter the cubicle Phoenix had pointed to. The room was dominated by a large unmade futon in the middle of the floor. Lydia hoped on the day she died that she would remember to make her bed that morning. Lydia had seen Jenny's work before, mostly close-ups of enormous pastel flowers that looked like female genitalia, but her work had clearly gone in a surprising new direction. Leaning against the walls were her new canvases, dark paintings in a tattoo style. Twisting snakes, red roses, and big-breasted women covered the canvases. The art was odd and disturbing, and it made Lydia wonder about the hidden corners of Jenny's life.

She picked up a framed photograph of Jenny from the side table. It showed her sitting and hugging a golden retriever. She looked happy to be alive, although that could just have been the artificial pose. Lydia set the photograph back down gently. Feeling like a sneak, she checked the desk drawers and side table quickly for a diary, but she couldn't find one. Jenny had probably kept her calendar and notes on the computer, but Lydia knew Phoenix would get suspicious if she turned it on. Besides, the police had probably combed the place already for evidence. If there were any clues in her room as to who the murderer was, Lydia was too oblivious to figure them out.

Lydia wandered back out into the main room, where Phoenix was now scarfing down some cold pizza while watching MTV videos. "I was wondering where Jenny had been working."

"She was waiting tables at Just-a-Cuppa—that new coffee shop on Bushwick—and painting in her spare time."

"Was she seeing anyone? I thought she mentioned a new friend."

"She told me she was dating someone really righteous. She'd been going on GotAnything for like a year now, and I guess she finally met someone there."

Perhaps Jenny had found a little happiness before she died. Lydia hoped so, anyway. She decided to improvise and see if she could uncover any dirt. "I heard she had some trouble with an ex one time."

Phoenix shook his head. "I don't think so. Where did you hear that?"

Lydia shrugged, hoping she wasn't making him too suspicious. "Just around. Maybe I heard wrong."

"Jenny wasn't the type to make enemies that way. She usually kept her exes as friends." Phoenix took a large swig of Red Bull and belched. "We're having a service for her tomorrow at dawn in Central Park, if you're interested."

Monday morning at dawn was an odd time for a service. Lydia was intrigued. "In the park?"

"Yeah, it's a goddess thing."

As Lydia scribbled down the details, she wondered if Jenny had been some sort of pagan. She wasn't sure how that fit in with the tattoo art, or if it had somehow contributed to her death. She thanked Phoenix for his help, then went back downstairs, leaving him to his nutritious meal. As she unlocked her bike, she mulled over what she had learned. Jenny and Marie seemed completely different, which made it even more baffling that they'd been chosen as victims one and two by a serial killer. Marie had excited strong emotions in almost everyone and appeared to have made plenty of enemies. Jenny seemed to have been a nice girl whose dark side was confined to her art. They had once been roommates, but that was years ago. Lydia wondered what had connected them in the killer's mind and why he had linked them to her photographs. She couldn't help feeling there was something she'd missed that linked the two women together.

She decided to stop by Just-a-Cuppa and ask around. Maybe a

strange man had come in recently and harassed Jenny. If she didn't turn up anything new, at least she'd get a cup of coffee out of the trip.

Just-a-Cuppa occupied a former garage and was trying very hard to be hip. The sofas and chairs looked like they had been hauled off the street on garbage pickup day before the trucks got there, and the beat-up bookcases sagged and leaned against one wall. The art on the opposite wall was of Indian goddesses, but it was painted so flatly in pink, oranges, and purples that it resembled paint-by-numbers canvases. Two earnest female college students tapped away on their laptops. Lydia hoped the coffee was better than the decor as she went to the mosaic-covered counter to order a cappuccino.

An enormous woman with a pierced tongue, lip, and eyebrow began preparing her drink. "I was wondering if you knew Jenny. . . ."

"Shit, yeah. We're like family here." The woman sneered. "This city is messed up."

Lydia nodded. The city felt strange and off-kilter to her right now, too. "I heard she had just hooked up with someone special lately online and I was wondering if you had met him."

The woman looked at her thoughtfully for a moment. "Are you from the police?"

Lydia considered lying, but she decided she couldn't pull it off. She shook her head.

The woman took out a cloth and began to clean the counter, a piece of glass over a mosaic of broken glass. "We don't gossip about our partners here."

Lydia wanted to ask right out whether or not Jenny had been a lesbian. The vibe in the café certainly pointed in that direction, but the pierced woman had already decided not to tell her anything.

She was pretty sure Phoenix had said that Jenny had met a man on GotAnything, though, so she dismissed it from her mind.

The coffee shop was definitely a dead end. Fortunately for Lydia, they made a very fine cappuccino. Lydia retreated to a reasonably comfortable armchair, hoping it had been deloused, and perused the bookshelf nearby. The books were mostly feminist literature and lesbian treatises, with a few pieces of erotic women's literature thrown in. Not a single detective story or noir classic to keep her occupied. Disappointed, she quickly finished her cappuccino and left.

Chapter 20

A strange mist eerily caressed the tops of the trees as the sun began to rise. The mood was just perfect, Lydia felt, for a morning ceremony involving witches and warlocks. She walked sleepily with Georgia Rae through Central Park, holding a map and feeling a little too much like a tourist. The grove of trees they were looking for was located in the Ramble, near the lake in the park, and neither one of them knew the park very well. Lydia was beginning to think that they would never find the right place, but then she spotted a group holding incense and candles.

"That's got to be them."

"Either that or a satanic ritual," Georgia muttered, shivering.

Lydia and Georgia walked up and stood awkwardly at the edge of the circle. An earnest-looking woman with brown braids and a tie-dyed robe stepped forward with a pitcher of water. "Please wash your hands and enter the circle." Lydia held out her hands and the woman poured water on them. She quickly shook her hands off and stuck them back in her pockets before they froze.

There was a shrine set up nearby with Jenny's photograph on it and a vase of carnations next to it. People murmured among themselves, and she wondered if anyone was going to speak about Jenny.

"I wish we'd brought candles," Lydia whispered to Georgia. "It's like that time I wandered into a pro-union demonstration and I was the only one without a pig nose or a sign."

Georgia stifled a giggle that came out sounding like a snort. "There's a pile of them over there. I'll get us some." Georgia quickly went and fetched two candles and lighted them on a neighbor's incense stick. She handed one to Lydia, who smiled gratefully. Holding it not only helped her blend in; it also gave her something to do with her hands.

The slightest taste and smell of spring was in the air. Lydia spotted the tops of the crocuses just beginning to push through the dirt. The trees were bare and gray and made a solemn backdrop for the service. She was grateful that the warmth of the crowd and the heat of the candle helped ward off the chill.

Lydia spotted a few familiar faces, but mostly she saw strangers in the crowd. Jenny's roommate Phoenix and some other guys were standing gravely in a group, looking glassy-eyed and stoned. The enormous pierced woman from the coffee shop was there with a group of women who were also large. The parts of them not covered in black leather were covered with tattoos and piercings. Lydia couldn't see Emily anywhere, and she wondered if she was coming.

"I checked out the GotAnything site last night."

Georgia raised one plucked and hennaed brow. "You're looking for a boyfriend?"

"No. I've just heard about the site a lot and I wanted to see what it was like. Jenny's roommate told me she'd met someone there." Lydia told Georgia about how the site promised a boyfriend in every bed and happiness in every apartment, but it wouldn't let her look at profiles unless she signed up for the service. GotAnything required an initial fee of one hundred dollars. She didn't have lots of money to spend, but it was the only lead she had at the moment. She had reluctantly taken out her credit card and typed in the numbers. She knew she was probably going to regret it when the bill came, but that would be fifteen days from now. Right now, she was willing to give all her worldly possessions to catch the guy.

Lydia had scrolled through the listings but had not been able to find a profile for Jenny or Marie anywhere. "It was really creepy to be looking for Jenny's profile under 'Women Seeking Men.' Somewhere out there, guys could be looking at Jenny's hopes and dreams and fantasizing about her as their wife. I doubt the Web site people keep tabs on the obituaries and remove the profiles. I think they probably just wait until the bill is thirty days past due."

Georgia looked like she wanted to say something but then stopped herself.

"I know it seems far-fetched," Lydia said. "But Jenny met someone online right before she was killed, so the timing could be right. Maybe the killer is one of those sickos who uses the anonymousness of the Internet to prey on the innocent, and maybe Marie found him there, too."

She told Georgia that when she couldn't find a listing for Jenny, she'd wondered if Jenny's could be one of the listings that didn't have a photo attached. A lot of the people used nicknames to keep everything anonymous, so she wasn't able to identify her from the remaining choices. The anonymity was liberating for some, but in this case, it might have become dangerous. In the end, she gave up in frustration. There was no way, without finding their profiles, to even begin to figure out if they'd both met someone through the site.

"That's okay. It probably was a dead end," Georgia said. Lydia opened her mouth to say something else, but just then the woman with the braids and another equally earnest-looking woman with a giant Afro and an African wrap dress moved to the center of the circle with a large roll of paper and a bag of pens. They spread out the white paper on the ground and began to draw on it. A few minutes later, the woman with the braids approached Lydia and Georgia.

"If you would like to write or draw your remembrances of Jenny or send her any messages from your heart, you're invited to do it on the paper." Georgia and Lydia each accepted a pen, and Georgia moved off to start writing on the paper. Lydia lingered.

"This is such a great idea!" Lydia told the woman with the braids. "Jenny and I moved in the same circles, but I wish I had known her better."

"She was totally awesome. We were in school together, and she really helped me get my head on straight." The woman was as earnest as she looked.

"Is her partner here?" Lydia asked, looking around the crowd as if she was straining to see someone. "I really wanted to pay my respects."

"You didn't know?"

"Know what?"

"Her partner was murdered just before she was. Everyone thinks it was the same killer."

Lydia stared at her openmouthed. She could barely comprehend what the woman was saying. "You mean Marie LaFarge?"

The woman nodded vigorously. "Did you know her? It was just

the most terrible thing. I swear, I haven't walked alone after dark since I heard."

"I thought they were just roommates," Lydia said, wondering if this woman even knew what she was talking about. Marie had been Lydia's friend. She'd assumed from the various men that Marie dated that she was heterosexual. But if Marie had been bisexual or a lesbian and had not trusted Lydia enough to tell her, then how good a friend had she really been?

The woman in braids was looking at Lydia uncertainly, probably trying to gauge from her expression whether or not she was some kind of homophobe. "They were, but then they realized recently that they were in love." She tossed her braids defiantly, daring Lydia to say something negative. "It's heartbreaking that they didn't have more time together."

Lydia turned away, not sure what to believe. She'd wondered briefly if Jenny had been a lesbian when she saw the café where she'd worked, but she had assumed from Phoenix's comments that Jenny had been heterosexual. But even if Lydia had known, she never would have guessed Jenny had been dating Marie.

She wondered if the Marie she had known was only an illusion. Marie had acted like her life was an open book, but she had been hiding some pretty big secrets. The new information certainly shot her theory of an online-dating killer out the window. Homophobic hate crimes and star-crossed lovers hardly seemed to fit.

As the woman with the braids wafted through the crowd to continue spreading her message, Lydia decided to write something to Jenny on the paper. She hated writing the same dull phrases that everyone inevitably wrote on greeting cards and in yearbooks. The situation seemed to call for something profound and serious, but she really hadn't known Jenny very well. She stepped up to where the paper was laid out and stood there for a moment, contemplating the way the bare branches of the trees moved against the sky. She saw so few trees in her own neighborhood that Central Park seemed like a country oasis. There was something peaceful about nature, but also something sinister lying in the bare points of the branches, like a skeleton's grasping fingers.

Lydia knelt on the grass and picked up a felt-tip pen. Choosing a spot next to a rainbow someone had drawn, she wrote carefully, "Jenny, you did not die alone or without friends. We will find who did this so you may rest in peace." And she signed her name with a flourish. Take that, killer, she thought to herself, pleased by her own bravado.

Georgia returned her pen to one of the women and came back to give Lydia a hug. "I need to go. I have a guy coming to fix that clogged sink at the salon."

"Okay. I'll see you later, then." It wasn't until Georgia had disappeared in the mist that Lydia thought to ask her what she'd known about Marie and Jenny. A drum circle had started up under a tree, with Phoenix taking the lead. A woman had begun to dance around and play a flute very badly. The strong smell of the sandalwood incense was beginning to give Lydia a headache, and she wished she'd left with Georgia. She had been to too many funerals in the last few days. At her age, she should be going to weddings and baby showers, not witnessing this parade of death.

Chapter 21

After Jenny's service, Lydia felt too restless to go straight back to the office. She thought about going to one of her favorite vintage stores to shop, but that felt too shallow. She needed to do something to help. She needed to find out who was killing her friends and models. But where to start?

On the subway, she idly watched the other people on the benches. She liked to play a game where she looked at someone's shoes and tried to guess what they did for a living. Some were easy. Paint-splattered Timberlands belonged to a construction worker. Black tasseled loafers belonged to a banker. She never found out whether or not she was right, but the game was fun nonetheless. Looking at one woman's high heels reminded Lydia of her photographs. She had found what she needed to know about the clothing of the victims in the book *Lost Girls.* She had never met the author, Diana Gryziec, and she wondered what she was like. She must be an elderly woman now, since she had begun writing in the early 1970s. If the police had been able to locate her, there was no reason that Lydia couldn't do so, as well.

As soon as Lydia hopped off the subway at Bedford Avenue, she saw a little Polish pharmacy on the corner and went in. The woman behind the counter had bleached-blond hair and was carefully applying magenta lipstick. Lydia knew better than to interrupt anyone in the middle of such a delicate operation. She waited patiently until the woman had covered every inch of her lips and delicately dabbed off the excess before she asked her question.

"Could I borrow your phone book for a moment?" The woman nodded and handed it over. There were benefits to being a regular customer, and one of them was trust. They could always ask her what had happened to their phone book the next time she came in for shampoo if she didn't return it right away.

Lydia paged through the white pages under *G.* There were a few Gryziecs, but none with a *D* and none in Williamsburg. They were all down in the Brighton Beach area. Suddenly, she remembered that Romero had told her another name. Diana Randolph. Perhaps she had gotten married since writing the book. Lydia flipped over to the *R*'s in the book and ran her finger down the page. There were a lot of them, but only one *D,* listed on South First Street. Lydia dialed the number and hastily hit SEND before she lost her nerve.

The phone rang and rang. Lydia was just about to give up, when a quavering voice answered. "Hello?"

"Hi, this is Lydia McKenzie. . . ." She found it hard to know where to begin. She had so many questions.

"I know who you are." The voice got stronger. It was bold, brassy, and had the bite of a native Brooklynite.

"You do?"

"Sure. The cops came to visit and were convinced that I knew you. But I don't get out as much as I used to."

Lydia had too many questions bubbling up in her brain that she was dying to know the answer to. "Do you think I could meet you this morning? I could take you out to coffee."

"Bring me the coffee here and you've got a deal. Milk, two sugars. Bell number four."

Lydia hung up thoughtfully. She left the phone book on the counter in front of the blonde and thanked her. The blonde made no move to take it, since she was now painting her nails a deep purple. Lydia walked over to Dave's coffee shop to get a cappuccino and a regular coffee for Diana. She decided to splurge on two muffins, as well. She was suddenly hungry after her early morning wake-up and realized she had had nothing to eat yet.

She went to South First Street, sipping her coffee and trying not to rip into her bag of muffins. It would be much more polite to wait and share, she reasoned. She was so curious to meet Diana, and she didn't know what to expect. She guessed Diana would have an interesting edgy quality, since she had a fascination with the unidentified dead of Brooklyn, as well. The woman observed clothing through the blood and gore and gave the lost girls their humanity again.

A flash of pink in a passing car reminded Lydia of Emily and her pink coat. She suddenly remembered that Emily hadn't ever come to the service. She took out her cell phone and looked to see if she had any messages. There were none. She quickly dialed Emily's cell phone.

She left a message on Emily's voice mail. "Hey, it's Lydia. I was just wondering where you were. I left you a message yesterday about Jenny's service. Call me as soon as possible or I will start to get very worried and call the police. Bye." Lydia closed her phone and frowned at it. Emily was a big girl and could take care of herself, but she expected her to be a little more considerate. It wasn't fair to leave friends hanging and wondering if you were all right.

Lydia had reached Diana's apartment house. She obediently rang bell number four and waited. Peering through the glass window, she could see black-and-white-tiled floors and walls painted a strange aqua color. Perhaps the paint had been on sale the week the building super needed to redecorate. Then she heard a strange tapping sound, faintly at first. The sound grew stronger, until finally a small woman using a white-tipped cane came into view. She was using the cane to feel for the next step. Lydia took a deep breath and felt her eyes fill with tears for a moment. The woman who had given so much by her observations was blind now.

Diana opened the door without any fumbling. "Well?"

"I'm Lydia—I just called you."

Diana's eyes shifted to where Lydia was standing. The woman was wearing black silk pants and an interesting Chinese-style blue jacket. Her hair was white and thick and caught back in a ponytail. "Come on in. You have my coffee?"

Lydia nodded, and then reminded herself that Diana couldn't see her. She cleared her throat. "Yes, I do.'

"Good. Bring it up." Lydia followed behind Diana as she tapped up the stairs. She moved pretty fast for a blind woman. She stepped neatly over a broken tile on the outside of the fourth stair, which could easily have tripped her. Lydia would have found it difficult to remember this woman was blind if it weren't for the cane.

Diana opened four locks to get inside her apartment. Lydia supposed the woman had seen enough murder to know the dangers of having an easily accessible apartment. Inside, the place was neat and spare. Lydia guessed a real estate agent would call it a "junior one bedroom." The kitchen wasn't much more than a corner, but it looked well used. Something felt odd about the space, and it took Lydia a few moments to realize that there were no pictures on the walls or objects on most of the surfaces. Since Diana was sightless, neither would have given her much pleasure.

"Nice place," Lydia said. She wondered how she kept it so clean. She hoped she had some help.

"It is just the right size for me. If it were too big, I would never be able to find anything. Let's sit down and have our coffees. Would you like a real cup?"

Lydia almost said no, but then she decided that since Diana probably wanted one, she would say yes. "Okay. Can I get them out?"

"No, no." Diana was already at the cabinet, lifting down two large white modern mugs. "But it would be helpful if you poured. I dislike getting burned." Lydia poured the coffee into mugs. She waited, not sure if she should hand Diana hers. Diana answered the question by feeling along the surface of the table until she found the mug. She took it in her hand and walked steadily over to an easy chair. Lydia followed her and sat down in another chair.

Diana took a moment to smell her coffee before taking a sip. "Ah, Dave's coffee. My favorite." Lydia's jaw dropped. She had heard that when you were blind, your other senses were made more sensitive, but she'd never witnessed this herself.

"That's amazing you can tell."

Diana let out a long throaty chuckle. "It was actually just a lucky guess. I wish I could see your face!"

Lydia smiled, glad she couldn't. She was a little too perceptive for Lydia's comfort.

"When the police called about my book, I realized it had been years since I'd thought about it. Tell me about your photographs."

Lydia tried to do so. She had lost so much of her earlier enthusiasm for her project that it was tough. She was reminded only of her lost friends and the terrible real violence that now permeated her art. She described the way she had used Diana's descriptions as springboards and had set the scenes in the neighborhood. "I wish I could show them to you. I would be interested to know how close they were to the originals."

Diana shook her head. "No staged death can come close to the real thing. You would never have wanted to see what I saw, or what the police see. It haunts you forever. I wrote the book to exorcise those images, but I'm still visited at night by ghosts. It doesn't matter that my eyes don't work; I can still see them."

"It made me so sad that all of the women in the book were never identified. That's what first attracted me to the project." Lydia began to tell her about her friend from elementary school, the one who had been kidnapped and killed. "The family only had peace when they knew what had happened to her."

Diana felt carefully for the side table and set down her coffee mug. "Not all the women went nameless. Not long after I published the book, one of the women was identified. It just so happens she was the one killed like Marie LaFarge."

Lydia sat up, her eyes riveted to Diana's face. "Who was she?"

"Her name was Carrie Lamott. She left her home in rural Pennsylvania just a month before her body was found. Her parents had looked for her and had notified the Philadelphia police, but they didn't think to look in New York City. They missed the notices when Carrie's body was found."

The woman had a name. Lydia felt as if a bolt of energy had been injected into her spine. "The family found her through your book?"

"That is what they told me. I was quite proud of that." Diana stared into space for a moment and then shook her head. "But finding out her fate didn't bring Carrie's family peace. I think they would have preferred to keep believing that someday she would come walking in the door."

"And the police never found the killer."

"No, they haven't. But the recent murders have reopened the case. The detectives who visited me were very interested in the murder of Carrie Lamott."

On Lydia's way to the office, she called Emily's cell phone again. When Emily still didn't pick up the phone, she couldn't help worrying. She called Georgia and Stuart. Neither had seen her or heard from her. Stuart thought that she might have gone to Vermont for a shoot. "Some lady wanted portraits of her twelve Labradoodles. It's one of those places that doesn't have cell phone service." Labradoodles, crosses between poodles and Labradors, had become all the rage, and cost a fortune.

Lydia was only slightly reassured. She thought Emily had understood that they were to be in touch with one another, so that no one would have no reason to worry. She tried not to panic, just in case Emily really was just away on business, but she was caught between anger and fear. She didn't think Emily would have ignored Jenny's service if all were well.

She wondered how Romero was using the information about

Carrie Lamott in his investigation. Perhaps he was linking the murders together and was hot on the trail of the killer. She wished she knew him well enough to ask, but she had to be content to hope he'd catch the guy before it was too late for Emily.

Chapter 22

After an early-morning funeral, the anxiety over Emily, and what felt like a long day dealing with corporate phone records at the office, Lydia was beyond grumpy when she finally got home. The lock on the front door of her apartment building was still broken. Her mailbox was hanging open again, with her mail sitting there for anyone to grab. She removed the mail tentatively, and was relieved, for once, to receive only a pile of bills and credit-card solicitations—no photographs. She hoped—no, prayed—that the killer was finished. Unfortunately, she doubted that was the case. He was too much of a blackguard to be satisfied.

She wished she had enough money to move to a better apartment in the neighborhood. Rents had been climbing steadily over the past couple of years, and the luxury-condo market was far out of her reach. Occasionally, when she carried home heavy groceries, she daydreamed about how nice it would be to have an elevator.

She walked wearily up the stairs and stopped short in the hall. The front door of her apartment was standing open. Someone had broken in. Her heart pounding wildly, she stood frozen, too terrified to move. Someone had invaded her home. Either the person had robbed her and left or he was still there. Neither scenario was comforting. She needed help. With trembling fingers, she called Romero.

"Yeah?" He didn't sound pleased to hear from her, but she hadn't exactly been a bearer of good news lately.

"My apartment door is standing open. Maybe it's just a run-of-the-mill robbery. . . ." She realized that her voice was shaking. She leaned against the wall to steady herself.

"Have you been inside?"

"Not yet."

"Don't move," he ordered. "I'll be there in fifteen minutes. And I'll send a patrol car over immediately."

The police officers arrived a few minutes later. They were both skinny guys who looked like they'd graduated from the Academy about five minutes ago. The one with a blond crew cut had his hand permanently resting on his gun, as if he was afraid someone might take it. The other one had a mean expression, as if he hoped someone would give him a reason to use his nightstick. He'd probably taken his career as bully on the playground to the next logical step when he joined the force.

"Ma'am, what seems to be the problem?"

"My apartment . . . it was locked when I left," Lydia said, gesturing weakly toward her open door.

The rookies looked over the open door but didn't make a move. The blond rookie leaned over to the other one. "We're supposed to sit tight and wait for a homicide detective."

The belligerent one popped his gum impatiently and turned to Lydia. "Someone dead in there?"

"I hope not," she said wearily. She desperately wished she could crawl into bed and make all of this disappear.

The cops looked impatient to be off, but they stayed with her until Romero came up the stairs two at a time, looking worried.

Romero nodded to Lydia and turned to the rookies. "What's the situation here?"

"No one has entered the premises yet."

"Good." Romero nodded at the cops. "Let's go."

Lydia was happy to stand aside as they all advanced toward the open door, guns drawn. She had no desire to tangle with a criminal. This was definitely a job for professionals.

A few moments later, Romero emerged from the apartment, scraping a hand through his hair. "I'm sorry, but I need you to go in and take a look."

Lydia straightened up. "Has he been inside?"

Romero didn't meet her eyes. "I believe so."

Lydia followed Romero, her feet dragging. She knew she wasn't going to like what she saw. The killer was getting closer. Before, he'd been content just to use her photographs for his crimes. Then he had put a photograph in her mailbox to taunt her. And now he had invaded her home. She was afraid to find out what his next step would be.

She crossed the threshold of her apartment and for a moment forgot to breathe. The invader had hit her place like a whirlwind. Clothes were everywhere, books were off the bookcase, and her furniture was overturned. In the center of the living room was a large circle painted in what looked like blood, and sitting inside of it was a Polaroid of a woman.

"Is it . . . blood?" Lydia whispered. For someone who re-created death scenes, she was remarkably squeamish about blood. Doing black-and-white photography helped, but she usually tried to minimize the wounds in her photos and concentrate on the pose and mise-en-scène.

"It's just paint. I don't want the scene contaminated, but I want you to look and see if you recognize the woman in the photograph."

Lydia stepped forward, careful not to touch any of her ruined possessions, and looked down at the picture. The woman in the photograph was tied up and was looking at the camera with familiar, terrified eyes. All Lydia's fears had been realized. The killer had taken Emily.

Chapter 23

Despite the wool blanket wrapped around her, and the heat in the cop car turned up full blast, Lydia continued to shake uncontrollably. Emily was in terrible danger. She wanted to believe that the cops could rescue her, that she was somehow still alive and safe, but she remembered what he'd done to Marie and Jenny. No one was safe from this killer. He was capturing and killing her friends one by one. He had to be stopped.

The rain had ended and the street looked cleansed. Her neighbor Mrs. Zablonsky came by the police car. Lydia occasionally helped her carry her groceries upstairs and her trash downstairs. Mrs. Zablonsky stared at Lydia, who was sitting in the back of the cruiser, probably thinking she had been arrested. Great, now all her neighbors were going to think she was a drug dealer. She was definitely going to have to move.

Lydia had known that Emily was in trouble from the first voice message she had left for her. She should have marched down to the police station right away and thrown a fit until they helped look for Emily. She should have gone to Emily's loft and broken in to make sure she was okay. She should have done more. She could have done so much more.

She closed her eyes and rested her head against the back of the seat. She thought of her trashed apartment with a pang. The mess was minor compared to her fears for Emily, but it still loomed in her thoughts. Having her stuff destroyed was a horrible violation. Her sanctum had been desecrated. Her beautiful clothes and other possessions had been destroyed. She hadn't gotten a good idea of the damage, so there was no way of knowing if any of her stuff had survived the vicious attack. Tears threatened to spill down her cheeks again. She felt she was just a few millimeters away from total hysteria.

Romero came to the side of the police car and leaned in to speak to the cop in the front. The driver was a young black guy who looked like he wasn't long out of high school.

"You can take a walk around the block. Be back in ten minutes." The cop got out of the car and headed for the nearest bodega.

Romero slipped into the back next to her, holding a Styrofoam cup. "How are you doing?"

"I can't stop thinking about her," she said, squeezing the words out between chattering teeth. She felt like she'd cried so much in the past week or so that she'd completely drained her body. "She must be so scared." Lydia did not want to think about Emily dead. Emily kidnapped was bad enough.

Romero passed her the cup. "I thought you might be able to use this."

Lydia took a sip and winced as it burned her tongue. Hot, strong coffee slipped down her tight throat, heavy and sweet. She held the hot cup gratefully and felt herself calming down.

"We'll do everything we can, but we're not superheroes."

"I got a call the other day from Ron Jamison at the *New York Observer,*" Lydia told Romero. She had meant to tell him earlier, but she'd been afraid he would accuse her of leaking the news. Now she was willing to risk it to make sure he had all the facts he needed. "He knew about the photographs, everything. You might have a leak."

Romero shook his head. "He's playing with us. You need to be careful."

Lydia thought about all the damage the killer had done. He had stolen lives, and destroyed the peace in their community. It all seemed so senseless.

"I'm so worried about Emily. She's a wonderful person, and she doesn't deserve this."

"You should be worried more about yourself. He's after you."

Lydia shook her head. He had ripped her apartment apart, but he hadn't been there to grab her. "There's no way of knowing. . . ."

"He left a message for you up there."

Lydia shivered. She'd missed that, but she had been so focused on the photograph of Emily, she hadn't looked around much. "What did it say?"

Romero watched her gravely. "It said 'You're next.' "

Chapter 24

Lydia had no choice but to call Georgia to see if she could crash at her place. Her apartment was officially a crime scene and she had nowhere to go. Even if she could have stayed there, she wouldn't have been able to sleep. First of all, there was nowhere for her to sleep—her mattress had been cut up and splattered with red paint. But second of all, she couldn't rest there, knowing that the killer might come back at any time to finish her off.

She usually told her best friend everything, but she was keeping a lot of secrets from her these days. She couldn't tell Georgia why she wanted to stay with her, because Romero had warned her that telling anyone about the photograph of Emily might endanger Emily's life. The police were doing everything they could to look for her, but they didn't have many clues. Romero wanted Lydia to go to a safe house, but she knew she'd go crazy if she couldn't help look for Emily. Meanwhile, she told Georgia the simplest lie that she could to explain why she had arrived without any of her possessions.

"You were robbed?" Georgia said. "I knew you should have fixed those locks."

"I asked the super to do it, but he never got around to it." Lydia curled up on Georgia's couch, hugging a beer to her chest. She had always felt safe in her apartment, but now she probably never would again. Emily had probably felt safe in her life, too, and something far worse had happened to her.

"There's a serial killer on the loose. Just have the locks fixed and deduct it from your rent. That's the only way to deal with that deadbeat." Georgia was on a motherly roll. She liked to tell people what to do, whether they wanted to hear it or not.

Lydia took another sip of the beer and counted to twenty. The last thing she needed was a lecture about how she could have prevented the break-in at her apartment. Or stopped a psycho killer from using her art to kill her friends. A killer might come after her at any time, and all she had were a few piddly self-defense moves to stop him. Her life had turned into a nightmare, and she didn't want to make it worse by alienating her best friend. Life felt very short and precious these days.

Georgia's cell phone rang to the tune of "Georgia on My Mind," and after taking off all the pillows on the futon, they finally found it. Georgia was almost as bad as Lydia when it came to misplacing her cell phone.

Lydia swung her numb legs off the sofa and went to use the bathroom. Her legs felt wobbly and strange, but she didn't want to sit there and listen to Georgia talk on the phone.

After splashing water on her face and examining her bloodshot eyes in the mirror, Lydia reemerged from the bathroom. Georgia was standing in the kitchen with her hands on her hips. She had a look on her face that she had to have inherited directly from her mother. Lydia felt instantly guilty.

"What's the matter?"

"Stuart just called. He says that Emily is missing."

"When I called him before, he said she might be away on business." Lydia dug out a roll of Life Savers from her bag and carefully removed the one on top. She put it in her mouth, letting the warm buttery flavor wash down her throat.

"He went by her place. Her mail is stuffed in her mailbox, and her cat was hungry and thirsty. She never would have left without making arrangements for the cat."

"Stuart has keys to her place?"

Georgia nodded. "He's looked after her cat before. He said she should be home by now if she was going to do the job she mentioned."

Lydia bit her lip to prevent herself from blurting out that Emily had been kidnapped and was in danger.

But Georgia's eyes filled with tears. "Oh God. Do you think the killer could have gotten her?" Georgia sat down on the futon and dropped her head to her hands.

Lydia sat down next to her and gave her a hug. She needed the hug just as much as Georgia. "We were all afraid this could happen."

"I can't believe it. First Marie, then Jenny, and now Emily. When will it end?"

It would stop only when the killer was caught. So far, the only suspect the police had shown an interest in was Stuart. She'd originally thought the notion that Stuart was a killer was preposterous, but he'd had opportunity and a possible motive. Kidnapping Emily would have been a piece of cake, since he had keys to her place.

Stuart was someone she trusted. Marie had trusted him, too, and Jenny had probably thought of him as a nice quiet guy, just as Lydia had. He had a grudge against Jacques, and he had fought with Marie. But it still didn't explain why he would have killed her or Jenny, or used Lydia's photographs to do it.

Something had to connect the three women besides Lydia and her photographs. If only Lydia could figure out what it was, she might have a shot at catching the killer.

"Did you know that Marie and Jenny were a couple?" Lydia asked. Georgia was always up on all the gossip and it seemed odd that she wouldn't know.

Georgia avoided looking at Lydia, wiping her eyes with a balled-up pink tissue.

"Why didn't you tell me? I felt like such a fool when I found out. I actually thought Jenny had met a man on GotAnything," Lydia said.

"Marie asked me not to say anything. She said the fashion world was notoriously fickle and someone could use it against her. I think her parents were homophobic, too. They didn't even want to hear about her relationships."

After Jeanne Goldberg's reaction to being outed by a photograph, it made sense that Marie wouldn't have wanted to tell any of her business colleagues she was in love with a woman. But Lydia sorely resented being seen as only a colleague.

"I thought we were friends," Lydia said, wounded. "I wouldn't have gossiped about it or hurt her for the world." The slight was even more painful, since she was unable to ask Marie why she hadn't trusted her or to mend fences with her.

"She would have told you eventually, I'm sure. I only knew because I walked in on them at that party at Brian's a few months ago.

Jenny and Marie were kissing on his bed, tongues and everything. They jumped up when I came in, and I was completely embarrassed. When Marie asked me to keep quiet, I couldn't very well say no. In fact, it's one of the things I'm really proud of doing—keeping my word to her."

Lydia still didn't understand it. They lived in New York City, where gays and lesbians routinely strolled down the street holding hands. The city prided itself on cutting down on hate crimes, and most people were too busy to worry about someone else's sexuality. It wasn't right that they'd felt they had to cover up their relationship and keep it from friends.

"Does Emily know about their relationship? Is she a lesbian, too?"

Georgia shook her head. "Everyone knows she is in love with Stuart."

Lydia had assumed that was true, but finding out about Marie and Jenny's relationship had shaken her confidence in her intuition. Perhaps Emily's confidence in Stuart had been misplaced, too.

Georgia jumped up and started to pace around the living room. "I can't believe Emily could be lying in some dark alley dead while we sit here gossiping and drinking beer!"

Lydia put her beer down with a thump. "We need to think through this calmly and figure out how to help her."

"I guess we could call everyone she knows. That way, we can figure out where she is and if she's in any danger."

Lydia knew Emily was in danger, but calling people might help them figure out where she was last seen and if she was worried about any individual. There was nothing else they could do. They both went through the phone listings on their cell phones, looking for people who knew Emily. They split the list and both began dialing.

Lydia called Rain and Georgia called Dina at the hair salon. They would both know a lot of people who knew Emily, too

Rain, although not a very helpful person, was frequently in the darkroom. She told Lydia she had seen Emily there on Friday morning. "She seemed really distracted about something," Rain said. "I just assumed it had to do with Marie's and Jenny's deaths."

"Did she say anything specific to you?"

"She asked me whether I knew if Marie had kept a calendar of some kind."

Lydia suddenly felt light-headed. What could have been in Marie's calendar that Emily wanted to see? She had gone through it carefully herself and it had not revealed anything significant, just appointments with her clients. Emily might have just wanted to expand her freelance contacts, but she could also have been looking for any mention of Stuart. Lydia was glad she'd mailed it to Romero. She wondered if he had discovered anything in it.

A few phone calls later, they concluded that no one had seen Emily for several days, and their questions had caused general alarm among their friends. They all feared the worst. There was a serial killer targeting artists, and any one of them could be next on the hit list. Their safe world had been violated.

Georgia powered up her laptop while she talked on the phone and sent a few E-mails to people she hadn't gotten on the phone. They wanted to make sure as many people as possible were looking for Emily.

"Do you mind if I check my E-mail?" Lydia asked. "I wasn't able to do it today."

Georgia nodded and got up. Lydia logged in and scrolled down, deleting the usual number of junk E-mails. There was nothing that couldn't wait until the next day. And there was no word about Emily.

Exhausted, she stepped away from the computer. Her vision was starting to blur as the adrenaline and caffeine wore off. She helped Georgia pull out the futon bed in the living room and make it up with flowered pink sheets—a gift from Georgia's mother, who adored Laura Ashley. Georgia slept on bright orange silk sheets and sneered at her mother's taste, but she refused to throw away good sheets.

Lydia washed the grime of the city from her face, changed into one of Georgia's T-shirts, and fell into bed. She was bone-tired, but she couldn't get her eyes to close. She told herself it was because she was in a strange bed, but that wasn't all of it. She kept remembering Emily's scared eyes, the red paint spread across her ruined apartment, and the ominous message from the killer. Was he really planning to kill her next?

Chapter 25

As the sun peered through Georgia's blinds, Lydia decided there was no way she was going into the office. While she still had her gruff morning voice, she left a message on the D'Angelos' machine that she felt too sick to come in. They would have to find some way to live without her. She had more important things to do first thing in the morning than sit in the office waiting for the phone to ring. She had to search for Emily. She and Georgia had made arrangements to meet Stuart at Emily's loft at nine o'clock.

Georgia staggered into the kitchen at eight to start a pot of coffee. She looked like she'd slept as little as Lydia. Once this whole mess was over, they were definitely going to have to check themselves into a spa or something. Not one of those places that made you eat sprouts, but somewhere that had hot springs and even hotter studs giving massages. Meanwhile, she would have to settle for a hot shower and clean clothes.

She borrowed gray wool pants and a green tunic sweater from

Georgia. She felt strange wearing Georgia's clothes. Neither piece fit exactly right, but at least they were clean and presentable. Her outfit standards were definitely dropping under stress.

Stuart was waiting impatiently next to his motorcycle when they arrived at Emily's loft building.

"Have you heard from her? Did you call the police?" Stuart had dark bags under his eyes and looked like he hadn't slept in days.

"Let's see what we can figure out from her loft, okay?" Lydia didn't want to endanger Emily's life by revealing just how worried she and the cops were about Emily.

"Do you realize what can happen to a vulnerable woman alone in the city?" Stuart's voice sounded almost hysterical. He wasn't at all his normal placid self. If he was innocent in all this, Lydia sincerely hoped he was discovering how deeply he cared for Emily. If he was guilty, Lydia knew this was going to be only the start of his suffering, because she would do all she could to make sure he paid for the crime. Georgia gave him a hug and steered him toward the door.

Lydia had been to Emily's loft before, but only for the occasional dinner party, never for a casual visit. Emily was a private person, and although she was always friendly with everyone, she had a deep level of reserve that was hard to breach. A white family had adopted her when she was a baby, but she was always reluctant to discuss race or how hard it must have been for an Asian kid to blend in someplace in upstate New York, where she'd grown up. Perhaps it was her yearning to belong that had inspired her high school cheerleading career. Lydia had never asked her, and now she might never find out.

"What are we looking for?" Georgia asked, wearily surveying Emily's messy space.

"Clues," Lydia said brusquely. "Calendars, notebooks, anything that might give us an idea of what was going on in her head before she disappeared."

"But what if she had no idea something was going on and was just randomly attacked?"

"Then we probably won't find any clues," Lydia said, but she was determined to look anyway. The killer wouldn't stop, she was sure, until the police had him behind bars.

Stuart looked uncomfortable as Lydia and Georgia began to go through Emily's desk and dresser drawers. He had called them in alarm, but now he was plainly having second thoughts. "What if she's just on a trip?"

Lydia did not like going through Emily's underwear drawer, either, but Emily's life was on the line. She wanted to tell them about the photograph of Emily that they'd found in her apartment, but she couldn't do it. If Stuart was the killer, she had to do everything possible not to let him know what was going on.

"You said she always called you before she went anywhere."

"I know. Maybe she just forgot," he said. "I was just wondering what she would think if she saw us now."

"Hopefully, she would be gratified by her friends' grave concern for her. Are you going to help us search or not?"

"Did you do this to Marie's place, too?"

Lydia turned and studied Stuart. He looked sick to his stomach. She suddenly remembered his argument with Marie before she died. She didn't know what it had to do with the murders, but it was important to figure out if he was upset about more than just Emily. He was a little too upset about whether she'd searched Marie's place.

She decided to go for the offense. "You mean did I find what you left at Marie's?"

"Yes," he said miserably.

"I don't know. Why don't you tell me what it was?"

"It's a long story."

"Could it have to do with Emily's disappearance?"

"I don't know," Stuart said. Emily's cat purred and rubbed against his leg. Her bowl had been empty when they arrived, and Stuart had fed her. Now he picked the cat up and buried his face in her calico fur.

"I feel bad because Emily and Marie argued right before Marie died and it was all my fault." Lydia was beginning to lose track of all the people Marie had been fighting with before she died. Georgia, Jeanne, Stuart, and now Emily.

Stuart had Lydia's full attention now. "What about?"

"I, uh, borrowed some camera equipment from a client awhile back. I meant to return it, but then I didn't work for him again for months. Then I found out he'd claimed it as stolen when he spoke to his insurance company, and he collected the money for it. I couldn't very well bring it back then, could I?" Stuart shrugged helplessly, a gesture that some women would find irresistibly boyish. He looked irresponsible to Lydia.

Lydia didn't move a muscle as she waited for him to finish his story. He was justifying his theft, and he was worried about getting caught. That didn't make him a murderer, but it did make him a criminal. She remembered that he'd fought with Jacques over a supposed theft, too. At the time, she'd thought it was an unfair accusation, but now she was beginning to wonder.

"Marie saw the equipment at my place and guessed what had happened. She knew the client and recognized the stamp he used on all his equipment. She copied down the serial numbers in her calendar, as if she was going to turn me in. I was so scared. I begged and pleaded with her. I needed the client if I was going to stay in New

York. I realized later that she was just teasing me about it, but at the time I was really frightened. She took one of the tripods with her, saying I had to share with her in exchange for her silence."

Lydia remembered the odd numbers printed in Marie's calendar that she couldn't identify. "How did Emily become involved?"

"I told her about it one night when I got drunk. I was worried Marie would blab. She got mad at Marie and confronted her. She wanted her to return the tripod so I could give it back to the client and clear my conscience. But Marie just laughed at her and refused. And so Marie and I ended up yelling at each other, and that was the last time I saw her."

Stuart looked really miserable. Marie had loved to tease, and Lydia doubted Marie would have actually turned Stuart in. Marie would have strongly objected to having her loyalty or ethics questioned, and so perhaps the joke had become deadly serious. Stuart never would have worked again if he got the reputation for stealing his client's equipment. Had he killed to keep his reputation clean? Had he eliminated Jenny afterward because she'd found out about the theft?

Lydia was relieved that she wasn't alone with Stuart in Emily's loft. She stuck close to Georgia as they got back to their search through Emily's belongings for clues. Emily had noted on her wall calendar that she had work lined up in New York that week. Her answering machine was blinking, and a quick listen revealed clients bewildered by Emily's absence at their scheduled portrait appointments. According to the Labradoodle client, Emily had never arrived in Vermont. The evidence was sobering. Although Lydia had known full well her friend was in trouble, she realized she had hoped Emily would miraculously reappear.

While Lydia continued to search the desk, Georgia went through

Emily's closet methodically. Emily had never been much of a clotheshorse, preferring simple washable cottons to the latest trend. Georgia reached up onto the shelf and lifted down a tripod. Stuart darted forward. He grabbed it from Georgia, turning it over in his hands until he saw the serial number. Stuart went pale beneath his tan.

"It's the tripod Marie took. How did Emily get ahold of it?"

Lydia guessed that Emily had managed to snatch it from Marie's apartment in the course of arranging her memorial service. Her altruistic streak had been a total cover-up. No, Lydia didn't doubt that Emily had loved Marie and wanted her to have a wonderful service, but she had always been a little confused by Emily's enthusiasm for organizing the whole event. Emily had simply wanted to ensure that she had total access to Marie's equipment and calendar in an effort to protect Stuart. Lydia couldn't help but wonder if her interference would lead to her death.

Chapter 26

Lydia grabbed a slice of pepperoni pizza from a local joint. The pizza dripped with grease and it took about five napkins to soak it all up. She folded it in half to eat it so the sauce wouldn't slide onto the clothes she'd borrowed from Georgia. As she munched the pizza, she went over the facts that she knew so far. She had checked her cell phone repeatedly over the last couple of hours, but Romero had not called since the break-in. She guessed that meant that they hadn't found Emily. And unless they did find her body, Lydia wanted to believe there was still hope she was alive.

Stuart had looked shocked to see the tripod at Emily's house, and Lydia doubted that his surprise was faked. She liked Stuart, and she did not want to believe that her judgment of others was so flawed that she would be unable to recognize a murderer when she saw one. She didn't plan to go into any dark alleys with him alone, but she was also still actively looking for a more likely culprit.

The cops were staking out Box Street where Lydia had taken the photograph, and she had already searched Emily's loft. She didn't know what else she could do to find Emily but wait. It was about noon, and Lydia belatedly remembered that she had a job. If she didn't go in occasionally, she would end up getting fired and have no way to pay her rent.

Leo looked mildly surprised to see Lydia when she came in. "Are you feeling better?"

She'd forgotten that she'd called in sick. The piece of pizza sat like a lead balloon in her stomach and she couldn't decide if she really was going to be ill.

Leo grinned at her and pulled out a box of cannoli from a bag. "This will make you feel better. These are from Mama. She says she owes you."

Lydia made a face. Normally, a cannoli would be a dream come true, but she wasn't sure if her stomach could handle it. "I haven't done anything."

"No, but she told me you agreed to help us get rid of Heather."

Lydia had only promised to report Frankie's movements to his mother, not scare off bad girlfriends.

"I thought you said his feelings would fade with time."

"I changed my mind." The D'Angelos didn't fight much, and she guessed they hadn't forgiven each other for their last argument.

Lydia helped herself to a piece of the bribe and bit in. Covered in pistachio nuts, it was crunchy on the outside and soft and creamy on the inside. She decided it was perfect. Her stomach quieted and her conscience quieted, as well.

"What's your plan?"

"We don't know anything about Heather. Frankie is totally obsessed and won't hear a word against her. We'd like to have her shadowed and find out more, but I think she'd recognize me if I tried it." Leo bit into another one of the cannoli in the bag. Lydia did not understand how he stayed so thin.

"She lives in Manhattan?"

"From what she said, yes. But I can't find any record of her."

Lydia mulled it over. She would have leaped at the chance to go on an exciting stakeout just a week ago. But her life had become far too exciting lately. "She's seen me a few times, too. We've even worked together. How do you know that she won't recognize me?"

"I thought you'd be able to fade into the woodwork enough for her not to notice you."

The thought was a bit lowering for a woman who dressed to be noticed.

"How would anyone find her if you don't know where she lives?"

"She told Mama that she religiously goes to some yoga place on Sixteenth and Third Avenue on Mondays, Wednesdays, and Fridays from one to three. She was trying to get Mama to try it, too," Leo scoffed.

Lydia found it amusing to imagine Mama doing the lotus position in her polyester pantsuit, but all kinds of people enjoyed yoga. People also apparently enjoyed all sorts of pain, just not Lydia.

Lydia chewed carefully. She wanted to help; she just didn't want to be the bearer of bad news. It wasn't like Frankie suspected anything anyway. He was in love. Leo and Mama were determined to prove Heather was all wrong for Frankie, and she hated to see him get his heart broken.

"You don't want to do it," Leo said flatly. "That's okay. I'll call someone else."

"I'm sorry. It's just . . ." Lydia's voice trailed off. She had no idea what to tell him.

"It's fine," Leo said, already dialing the phone. "Why don't you take the rest of the day off? You still look a little ill."

Lydia nodded, too shocked to disagree. She decided he must want her out of the office before he plotted his next move against Heather. She hoped Mama wouldn't be so mad that she would stop sending over cannoli.

As she left the office, her phone rang in one of her pockets. After a search through every available one, she finally found it in her coat. It was Georgia. "Have you heard anything?" Lydia asked.

"No, nothing. I just pulled out my calendar and realized we were supposed to go to that animal shelter arts benefit tonight."

Lydia cursed under her breath. She had no energy for socializing, but she usually tried not to miss the annual gallery show to benefit the shelter. It might also be good to get out with Georgia and see if they heard anything about Emily. Then she remembered the horrendous state of her clothes closet. "I don't have a thing to wear."

"We can dig something up for you. Or we can try dropping in at Catcher's Attic." The store was one of Williamsburg's biggest and trendiest vintage stores. Students from NYU routinely came out to the neighborhood just to shop there. The prices were higher than those at lots of other places, but Catcher's Attic had a little something for everyone in its giant loftlike space.

The idea of shopping added a spring to Lydia's step. "It'll have to be something on the cheap side."

"Don't worry. We'll find you something that'll make you feel like a queen."

Chapter 27

Lydia stood next to an extremely ugly sculpture made of bicycle tires and plaster, her cape over one arm and a purse on the other, waiting for Georgia to arrive at the shelter benefit. A customer had a bad dye-job crisis, and Georgia had to stay late and try to save the woman's hair from ruin.

She felt elegant in the cream-colored lace dress with three-quarter sleeves and a flared skirt that she'd found at the shop. She was wearing a pair of Georgia's flats. Unable to access her collection of tights and purses, she'd made do with panty hose and a small lace bag that Georgia loaned her.

She tried to not look at the ugly sculpture, the bent wheels poking out of garishly painted plaster with no rhyme or reason, but it was difficult to avoid it. Like so many of the masterpieces shown in the neighborhood, the piece did not work on so many levels. If she were to read the accompanying artist's statement, she was certain the underlying meaning or life philosophy of the artist would be spelled out for her. But she was impatient with art that needed long explanations to be understood. She hoped her own photographs worked both with the background information and without. She wondered with a pang if they would ever be shown again.

Mark and Trash, two artists she knew from the neighborhood, were standing by the drinks table, bragging about their latest shows. They'd known Marie and had come once or twice to the critique group. Mark did glow-in-the-dark skull paintings, and Trash did found-art sculpture, assembling trash in new and interesting ways. They were dressed like identical twin truckers, with baseball hats, T-shirts advertising cheap beer, and tight jeans. Lydia strolled over.

"Hey, did you like that show at P.S.1? I thought all that modernist crap was over, man. Why are they showing it?" Mark complained. After listening to his familiar diatribe, which basically was about his frustration in not getting any shows, Lydia left them to whine and went in search of some other friends. The room was steadily filling up with a lot of people Lydia didn't know. Some people looked a little familiar, but she didn't feel comfortable going up to them and starting a conversation.

Sipping her drink next to a large pink rubber dog, she spotted Pip studying a painting of layered architectural drawings. She thought about strolling over to say hello, but she didn't feel like hearing him spew about the show. She stepped neatly back behind the pink dog to wait for him to clear out.

"Is this a private hiding spot, or can anyone join you here?" Lydia whirled around. Brian, one of Georgia's former band mates, stood grinning at her, a huge red cast on one arm. He was wearing brown plaid pants and a hooded sweatshirt. His square dark glasses made him look a little nerdy, but he was a very cool drummer and graffiti artist. He had fallen in love with Georgia years ago. But Georgia had a weakness for bass players and bad boys and only wanted to be friends. Lydia liked him and felt sorry for his doomed crush.

"How embarrassing! I saw someone I wanted to avoid—but I'd love to talk to you. What's up with you?"

Brian held up his cast. "Not much. I had a freak accident just before the band broke up. This van ran me off the road while I was riding my bike and really messed me up."

"I'm so sorry to hear that. Will you be drumming again soon?"

"I hope so." Brian reached out with his good arm to touch Lydia lightly on the shoulder. "I was really sorry to hear about Marie."

"You knew her, too? She touched a lot of lives, I guess." Lydia felt the familiar sadness wash over her. She supposed it helped to talk about Marie, but every time her name was mentioned, it felt painful.

"I met her through Emily, actually. We're both from Ithaca, so we go way back."

Lydia peeked over Brian's shoulder but couldn't see Pip anywhere. She felt guilty ducking him. "I think I knew that once and forgot."

"Have you seen Emily lately? She hasn't been returning my calls."

Lydia wished she could tell him. She felt horrible lying to everyone, but she had to do her best to keep Emily safe. "Maybe she got tied up. She's been really busy." Busy getting kidnapped, but hopefully not busy getting killed.

"She owes me money and I really need it to make the rent." Brian tapped his fingers on his cast, always the drummer. "I wouldn't bother her if I didn't have to. I know she was really upset by Marie's death, since Marie was a big hero of hers and everything."

Lydia wouldn't have described Marie as Emily's hero exactly, but she could understand what Brian was trying to say. Marie had lived life in a way that many envied. Her freelance fashion career had been taking off in a major way, the gallery show of her photographs from India had been a big success, and she'd had lots of friends to share her joy for living. But someone had stamped out that joy and that life, and Lydia wished she knew who and why.

"It's kind of weird, though, because I heard Marie left her some money."

"Some money? Why?" Lydia had a hard time imagining that Marie had left a will, and she didn't understand why she would have left anything to Emily. She wondered if Romero knew about it.

Brian shrugged. He looked behind Lydia and his eyes lighted up. She knew exactly who was behind her.

"Hey, sugar," Georgia drawled, giving Brian a polite kiss on the cheek. "How's my favorite drummer?"

Brian blushed. "Okay."

"Excellent." Georgia turned to Lydia and gave her a more enthusiastic hug, probably already dismissing Brian from her mind. She really didn't mean to be cruel. Georgia just had no idea how smitten Brian was with her.

"Let's go get a beer. See you later, Brian," Georgia said breezily.

"Don't forget to tell Emily to call me if you see her," Brian told Lydia sadly, watching Georgia disappear into the crowd. Lydia gave his arm a squeeze before she walked away. The room was suddenly full of people and too crowded for Lydia's tastes. On her way toward the bar, she had to push by a woman who was wearing a strange puffy green minidress and had a large fur hat on her head, as well as a man dressed like he was about to depart on a safari. They both shot dirty looks at her.

Lydia caught up with Georgia finally on the other side of the room. She accepted a bottle of beer and took a sip.

Georgia scanned the crowd behind her. "Has anyone heard from Emily?"

Lydia shook her head. Coming here to try to find out about Emily was hopeless, but it had seemed like a better idea than sitting at home. But now in the midst of the crowd, she realized she was in no mood to socialize. She had done her part for the cats and dogs, and now she needed to figure out what to do next.

Chapter 28

Lydia had not intended to walk back to Georgia's alone from the opening, but the cold evening air felt good on her overheated cheeks. She was lost in thought when a red van turned onto the street with a squeal of its tires. The van came down the street toward Lydia at high speed, its high beams blinding her. The drivers in the neighborhood were all crazy, as far as Lydia was concerned, but she slowed down and kept an eye on the van. The muffler on it coughed and spat noisily. Just as the vehicle was almost abreast of her, it swerved suddenly and came up onto the sidewalk in front of her.

Lydia was outraged. The van had nearly hit her. The driver bailed out of the van and ran around the front of it. She hoped he was coming to apologize, but that seemed doubtful. He was either drunk or crazy, possibly both. Lydia wanted to give him hell, but she prudently turned and ran. Her shoes were not made for running, and he easily caught up with her, grabbing her arm roughly. He was wearing a ski mask, and he only grunted when she kicked his shin. She fought wildly, hampered by her skirt, and managed only to drop her clutch purse. The man was surprisingly strong, and he dragged her across the sidewalk to his van. Lydia squeezed out a feeble scream as he wrenched open the door at the back of the van and shoved her in. She cracked her head on the side of the van and fell forward onto something soft and warm. She pulled herself upright to turn around and fight back, but the man had already slammed the door shut and locked it. She frantically tried to open the door, when she realized what she had fallen onto was a person. She recoiled just as the van took off again, and she fell backward onto a hard object.

Lydia felt behind her in the dark and came up with what felt like a heavy tool. She clutched it to her chest, terrified. She decided she might be able to use it against the other occupant of the van. She waited, her heart beating loudly, for the other person to strike. But the person didn't move. She slowly pulled herself upright to survey the scene. The van took a hard right, nearly throwing her off balance again, but she managed to wedge her foot against the floor and her arm against the wall and stop herself from falling again. A little illumination from a streetlight came in through a window in front of the driver, and it fell across the body in the van. Lydia saw only a long piece of dark hair and a familiar pink duffel coat before she leaped up. She had found Emily.

Excited, she scrambled across the van toward her. "Emily, it's Lydia!"

Emily did not move. Bracing herself for the worst, Lydia gently lifted Emily's wrist out from under her coat. Her pulse was faint but steady. Lydia had managed to find Emily still alive. One worry down, and a million more to go. Emily could be horribly injured and near death. She had to get them out of the van while they were still in Williamsburg and had some hope of getting help. The van couldn't run every red light in town; the killer was going to have to slow down sometime. Her first order of business was to figure out how to open the door.

Lydia crawled toward the door with the tool, getting momentarily tangled in her cape as she did so. She straightened it out and began to feel along the side for the lock. Luckily, it appeared to be a simple push-button deal and she easily tackled the first part. Now she had only to open it, leap out of a moving vehicle with the unconscious Emily, and run for safety. The rescue operation seemed impossible, but she knew she had no choice. She could either attempt to escape or die the way Marie and Jenny had. She felt the adrenaline course through her veins. She had only to imagine she was Martina, her self-defense instructor, and do exactly what she would do. She only wished that she had Martina's big muscles.

Lydia lifted up Emily's head and chest as gently as possible and slowly began to move her toward the back of the van. Emily was quite a few inches shorter than Lydia and many pounds lighter, but the van was full of junk. Dragging Emily a couple of inches at a time took ages, but finally Lydia made it. Lydia cradled Emily in her arms, willing her to keep breathing as she waited by the door for a change in the van's speed. The driver zoomed around another corner and she let her shoulder crash into the door to save Emily's head from further abuse. She winced but held on tightly. The door opened on impact and Lydia suddenly found herself staring down at the pavement as the van sped steadily on. She twisted and braced her injured shoulder against the side to keep Emily and herself from falling out. The van was going too fast for her to think of getting them both—or even herself—out.

At last, the van turned and began to slow down. Lydia waited, holding on to Emily at the open doorway. They might get only one chance and she had to be quick and agile in order to escape. The van slowed down even more and Lydia braced herself. With a quick prayer, she leaped ungracefully to the ground, holding Emily's face against her chest. Lydia landed hard on her knees. She was afraid that Emily had landed rather hard, with only her coat to protect her, but at least no one's head had hit the pavement. She had no time to assess the injuries. She had to keep moving. The van was moving away, and she assumed the driver had not seen them escape. But she had to get them out of the road fast so he wouldn't spot them.

A quick glance around revealed they were in the middle of an industrial park, although nowhere that she recognized. She spotted a deep doorway in a factory building ahead of her and decided that was her best bet for a hiding place.

Using a strength she had no idea she possessed, Lydia took off, half-dragging Emily toward the building, and losing Georgia's shoes somewhere in the process. The ground was cold on her feet, but she had to ignore it. Panting, she pulled Emily the last couple of yards into the doorway and waited. The hiding place wasn't fantastic, but it was the best she could come up with under the circumstances. The good news was that it was dark, so it would be harder for their pursuer to see them. The bad news was that it was dark and the streets were deserted.

She examined Emily quickly. She was pale and appeared to be unconscious. Lydia had no idea if he had drugged Emily or beaten her or what, but she had no hope of reviving her. She had to find a way to get her medical help as soon as possible.

Lydia felt through her pockets. She had dropped her bag when the killer had grabbed her off the street, and her cell phone was inside it. She had never wanted her phone so much as at that very moment. But she was going to have to improvise on her own.

She heard the unmistakable sound of the van returning—she had noticed that his muffler had a way of skipping beats, a sound as recognizable as a tattoo. Lydia waited breathlessly. Emily couldn't fight off a killer, and probably she couldn't, either. She knew she had no hope outrunning him while she was dragging Emily with her. She hated to leave Emily alone and vulnerable, but her only hope was to lead the killer away from Emily's hiding place and try to find help. They were in the middle of New York City, after all. She shouldn't have to run too far before finding someone with a cell phone who could help her and summon an ambulance for Emily.

Lydia heard the sound of the van door opening and shutting. She waited for a moment, tucking Emily's pink coat inside the doorway to make sure she was completely hidden. She took a deep breath, and, with a short apology to her sore knees and bare feet, she took off. She was breathing heavily before she had run even half a block, and her lungs were burning. She promised herself that if she got out of this alive, she'd start running on a treadmill and begin wearing sensible clothes and shoes. She scanned the block as she ran, but it was dark and deserted.

The sound of the killer's footsteps echoed behind her. Lydia looked around frantically for help but saw no sign of it. At least he didn't stop to hurt Emily, she thought. And then she began to wonder what her self-defense teacher, Martina, would do in this situation. She would probably have fought off the killer before he stuffed her in the van, but it was too late for that. What had she said you should always do first? Lydia's mind was a blank as she went through her brief lessons in self-defense. Her mind didn't feel like it was getting enough oxygen or something. Finally, she remembered. She was supposed to scream.

Lydia let out a very short, wimpy shriek. She barely had any oxygen to spare for anything louder. But if she wanted to save her life, she was going to have to come up with something better than that. Suddenly, she remembered what she was supposed to yell, something that always made people come to help. She took a bigger breath and screamed again.

"Fire! Help me!" Screaming felt good. She was finally doing something besides running away. She turned the corner onto another street. This one was bigger and wider and had a few cars parked on it.

"Fire! Fire! Help me!" She yelled even louder than before. The blood was pounding so loudly in her ears, she couldn't tell if the killer was still chasing after her or not. She didn't dare look. She screamed again and again, her throat becoming hoarse, and finally she heard the most welcome sound she'd ever heard: sirens. She hoped they weren't rushing to some bank robbery, but coming to help her.

The NYPD's blue-and-white cruisers squealed around the corner and Lydia waved her arms at them frantically. The drivers screeched to a stop in front of her and leaped out with guns drawn.

"Killer following me. . . . My friend is hurt in doorway. . . . Please help me. . . . Detective Daniel Romero . . ." Lydia tried to speak between gasps for air but knew she wasn't making sense.

A female cop with a long dark ponytail looked into her eyes and took her gently by the arm. "What happened, ma'am? You say someone is chasing you?"

"He grabbed me in a red van. I got out, but he was on foot. My friend . . ." Lydia had to stop to take a breath.

"Where's your friend?

"She is in a doorway two blocks from here. I dragged her there after we jumped from the van. The killer came after me. He's wearing a ski mask." Two cops jumped back into a car and sped away down the street in the direction Lydia had indicated.

The cop helping her pulled out her radio. "The suspect is on foot near Johnson Avenue, or is back in a red van. I repeat, a red van." After confirming Lydia's name, she also announced that Lydia had been found unharmed.

A few minutes later, Romero pulled up in his unmarked car. He jumped out of the driver's seat, and Lydia found herself running toward him and into his arms. He grabbed her in a bear hug and she held on as tightly as she could, feeling safe for the first time in ages.

Chapter 29

At the hospital, there were forms to fill out and endless questions to answer. Nurses wrapped her ripped-up feet and gave her hospital slippers to wear. There wasn't much they could do for her sore knees. Lydia knew her body was going to be seriously hurting the next day. Romero was having a hard time proving that Emily's and Lydia's abductions were tied to his ongoing murder investigation, so another team of cops was trying to launch its own inquiries. Their abductor and his red van had disappeared, and there was an all points bulletin out to try to find them. Lydia gave all the details she could on the vehicle, but one van pretty much looked like any other to her. She also tried her best to describe her attacker, but he had been wearing a ski mask and gloves, so she couldn't even be sure of his skin color.

As another cop questioned her for the third time about everything she could remember, Lydia suddenly turned to Romero. "How did everyone find me? I lost my cell phone and couldn't call for help."

"A woman saw you get shoved in the van. She picked up your purse and gave the dispatcher your name. I heard it over the radio and rushed over. By then, there were reports of a crazy woman running through the industrial park yelling 'Fire,' and I knew it had to be you." Romero smiled tightly. He looked like he had actually been worried about her.

"I was lucky," Lydia said. "I'd like to thank her."

"You were smart. You made a scene when he grabbed you, and you dropped evidence so that someone would find out you were gone. You got out of the van with Emily in some kind of crazy James Bond maneuver and then ran to get help. I'd say you pretty much rescued yourself." Lydia was shocked to hear Romero praise her. She was convinced she was just a nuisance for him.

Romero took a deep breath. "But none of this would have happened if you hadn't put yourself in harm's way. Were you begging the guy to kill you next? It's lucky for all of us that he didn't pull over to the side of the road and murder both of you." Lydia found the harangue particularly painful, because she knew he was right.

It was lucky he hadn't killed them both. Lydia didn't like to agree with Romero on anything, so she did something unusual: she kept her mouth shut.

The investigator cleared his throat and tapped his pencil on the paper. "We have your purse here, Miss McKenzie, if you'd like to check the contents." Lydia took the tiny lace purse and opened it up. She had a twenty-dollar bill, her phone, and a roll of butter rum Life Savers. She unrolled one and popped it in her mouth.

The investigator wasn't finished. "Could you describe the back of the perpetrator's van for us?"

"Again?" Lydia took a deep breath. "It was dark back there. But I fell on something and picked it up. I think it was a hammer."

"The kind that you use on nails?"

Lydia nodded and, exasperated, wondered if there was another kind. The killer was probably safe inside his hole by now, while they went over what seemed like irrelevant details. A doctor, an Indian woman with short gray hair, came out of Emily's room, and Lydia jumped to her feet.

"Can you tell me how she is doing?"

"Are you a member of her family?" the doctor inquired. Lydia froze, wondering if she could claim a blood relationship with the obviously Asian Emily. A stepsister? An adopted cousin?

After a moment, the doctor shrugged. "She's going to be okay. There's no evidence of any injuries. She's exhausted, dehydrated, and hungry, and she's drifting in and out of consciousness right now. We're replacing her fluids and hope to get her back on her feet in the next few days."

"Thank you, Doctor," Lydia managed to whisper through her tears. She had feared that Emily's injuries were worse, that she'd been tortured or that she had been hurt by the leap from the van. She was glad she would soon be on the mend physically, but she wondered how long it would take for her to get over the trauma of the event. Lydia swore to herself that she would do everything she could to help her.

The doctor rushed away to another emergency as Lydia sat back down, her knees weak with relief.

Romero conferred quietly with a cop nearby. "The guard will be there twenty-four hours, right?"

"Yes, sir."

Romero then took Lydia by the arm and escorted her out.

"Is Emily still in danger?"

"We don't know if she can recognize this guy. Until we do, we're going to be very careful."

"What about me?"

"You should be very careful, too. You said he wore the ski mask the entire time, so you wouldn't be able to identify him. I'd recommend you continue staying with your friend."

The lace dress Lydia had just bought was shredded and stained with blood. She was going to have to throw it away. She couldn't go back to wearing Georgia's clothes, though. "I need to pick up some clothes from my place." She hoped there were some without any red paint on them. Her stuff seemed a minimal worry when a serial killer was running around trying to kill her friends, but she still cared about her vintage outfits. She had spent years putting together her collection, and she hated to think it was another joy that the murderer had ruined for her.

"I'll take you there, then." As they walked down the hospital corridor, Lydia realized her pain medication was starting to wear off. Her knees felt stiff and bruised, and Romero had to offer his arm for her to lean on as they made their way out to his car, which was parked in the loading dock. She felt like an old woman as she shuffled along in her slippers.

The exterior of Romero's car was dark blue and dull. The interior smelled like air freshener and cigarettes. He probably wasn't the only one who used the car, but it was hard not to associate the smells with him. As Lydia bent her aching body to sit down, she nearly sat on a substantial paperback book. She turned it over and was surprised to find it was *War and Peace.* "Is this yours?"

"Yeah, don't sound so surprised."

She admitted to herself that she didn't think of cops as the types to read classic literature, but she hated to sound like a bigot. "I'm sorry. Do you like it?"

"Sure. It's the second time I've read it. I thought I'd check out the new translation." Romero smiled at Lydia's stunned look. "My dad was a high school principal and my mother a librarian, so they always encouraged me to read."

"My parents were teachers, too." Lydia told him, amazed that they had that in common. "How did you decide to be a cop?"

"I had a cousin on the force. He was a hero to me when I was kid."

"So you ran out and signed up?"

Romero shook his head, steering the car around a woman talking on her cell phone in the middle of the street. "He was shot in the line of duty. I guess I went in thinking I was doing it for him."

Lydia sat back in the car and tried to ignore her sore muscles. She hadn't realized Romero had so many layers to him. She couldn't stop thinking about their embrace and what it had meant. Possibly nothing, possibly everything. Both of them appeared to regret the lapse, though. He had now probably guessed that she found him attractive, and she didn't like it. Or maybe he thought she was in dire need of saving. Either way, she wished the hug had not happened, but there was no way to undo it now.

Lydia's apartment looked as decrepit as always, especially in the dark. Incandescent pigeon poop covered the steps, since the super was too lazy to clean it. She stopped at the mailbox for her mail. The mailbox was still broken. Not even a police investigation could fix that problem for her. Romero shook his head as Lydia removed a huge quantity of bills from her box.

Romero broke through the police tape across Lydia's door and she opened it with her key. The picture in the center of the room was gone, but the red paint and piles of stuff were still there. She imagined they had been photographed and cataloged by the cops, but now it was her responsibility to clean up after the killer.

Lydia stepped through the debris to look for some clothes he had not destroyed. Her spring and summer clothes were safely tucked away in wardrobe boxes, so only her winter clothes had received a beating. She tried not to look at the clothes that had been painted or shredded, for fear she'd cry.

Romero's phone rang. "Yeah," he growled into the phone. He stepped into the kitchen to talk to his caller, leaving Lydia to pack up on her own.

She rooted around until she found a pair of clogs, then slipped them on. She ditched the hospital slippers in the trash can, and got down to business. She lifted down a suitcase from the closet and began to throw clothes into it. First she put in underwear, socks, and bras. Then she found a few pairs of pants and tops that were unharmed. This was not at all the way she liked to pack. Normally, she went over all the occasions she would need clothes for and designed a couple of unique looks for each event. Then she carefully packed each item needed in her case. This time, she was in survival mode.

As Lydia pitched in items from her dresser, she spotted the photographs from Marie's party. She had never gone over them with Emily, but maybe Georgia would recognize someone from the pictures. Lydia threw the envelope into her suitcase. Then she went into the bathroom to pack some toiletries, averting her eyes from the red paint smeared on her mirror. Eventually, when everything calmed down, she would have to clean this place up. But right now, she just didn't have the time and energy.

Romero finished his call and came back into the living room. "All packed?"

"Yeah. Enough for a couple of days." She just hoped they caught him by then.

"Where am I taking you?"

"To my friend Georgia Rae's. At North Ninth and Bedford."

Romero took the suitcase from her hand. She watched as he carried it out of the apartment and down the stairs. As she followed him, empty-handed, she thought that at least chivalry was not dead. It felt good to have a man do something for her for a change. But she didn't kid herself that it somehow meant something. It was his job.

Outside, an ominous-looking full moon was rising above the rooftops. Seeing stars in Brooklyn was almost impossible with all the lights of New York City overwhelming their shine. Occasionally, she could see Orion on an especially clear, pollution-free night. But the moon was almost their only link to the cosmos, and its presence tonight felt unsettling. She'd read that the crime statistics rise alarmingly on nights with a full moon. She'd have to ask Romero sometime when she wasn't afraid of becoming another statistic.

They rode all the way to Georgia's in silence. All the streetlights turned magically green for him, as if they sensed that he was coming. She saw cop cars pause and then go on red all the time, but she couldn't imagine Romero doing that unless it was an emergency. He seemed to be honest and to do things by the book. His only transgression was to park illegally and get away with it.

"Pull over here," she instructed him when they got to North Ninth. He pulled over and scrutinized Georgia's building.

"How's the security at her place? Is it adequate?"

Lydia nodded and got out of the car. As they walked to Georgia's door, she wondered if anyplace would have adequate security to satisfy him. Fort Knox? The Pentagon? The security was adequate enough for her needs. And she knew Georgia had upped the number of locks on her doors and put in a new gate after her experience with the stalker. The precautions had made sense at the time. Personally, Lydia hated to feel like she was hiding behind bars, and she'd never gotten around to doing the same. But look what her blasé attitude had gotten her. An apartment filled with ruined clothes and red paint.

"You don't have to come up," she began, but when Georgia buzzed her in, he pushed open the door and carried her suitcase up. Limping behind him, she was glad not to have to carry it.

"Thanks," she said at the door, feeling strangely like she was being dropped at her door by a date.

"Be careful," he said, giving a small wave to Georgia.

She watched him disappear down the stairs before she finally went inside.

Chapter 30

Lydia tossed and turned all night on Georgia's futon bed. No position was comfortable for her aching body, and she just couldn't stop thinking about the killer. Was it Stuart? If not, who was it? Why was he attacking her friends? Why had he gone after her? There was nothing she knew about anyone that was particularly damaging, nothing that a lot of other people didn't know already. She considered herself a pretty harmless and reasonable person, so it was horrifying to find herself on someone's short list of people to get rid of. When she finally drifted off to sleep, her mind was haunted by dreams of being tossed in a red van and finding Emily dead this time. She woke in a sweat, and tossed and turned again until dawn.

Caffeine was the only thing keeping her upright the next morning. She threw on some clothes from her suitcase and for once didn't agonize over how she looked. The black wool pants and the forest green twin set conveyed no particular message. She needed to be clothed today, and that was as far as she was willing to think about the process.

Georgia had fussed over her a little the previous night when she had come in, but Lydia was so stoic, she'd backed off. But now that Georgia could see the dark circles under Lydia's eyes, she suggested that she go back to bed.

"I'm going into work today."

"Surely they would give you a day off if they knew you almost died last night." Georgia sounded shocked and annoyed. She would probably have liked nothing better than to fuss over Lydia all day and force-feed her liquids. But Lydia had no desire to be treated like an invalid. She was determined that her life should return to normal. Anything less meant that the killer had won this round.

Lydia did not want the D'Angelos to know she was messing around with a murder case. Their policy was quite clear when it came to interfering with open homicide investigations: They didn't do it and didn't want her even to think about it. But she also wanted a sense of normalcy. She wanted to be with someone who didn't look at her every couple of seconds searchingly to see if she was going to fall apart and needed a shoulder to cry on.

She wasn't planning to work all day, though. Lydia needed to go and visit Emily as soon as the doctor allowed her to. She was also determined to figure out who the kidnapper and killer was. He had used her photos, killed her friends, and tried to murder her, too. She needed to stop him before he tried to kill again.

She wished she could put to rest once and for all the idea that it was Stuart. She wondered if she could trap him into revealing his guilt. She dialed his number thoughtfully. But any real notion of trapping him went out of her head when she heard how he had spent his day.

"I should have stuck around to make sure Emily was okay, but instead I went to an outdoor photography seminar at the W Hotel all day yesterday. I thought a distraction would help, but I still worried about her."

Stuart's alibi could easily be checked if he was in a seminar. Someone would be able to confirm that he'd been there. If he had not grabbed Emily and Lydia, then he had not killed Marie and Jenny or attacked Jacques. She was happy to know that her original assessment of Stuart's character was correct, and that he wasn't the murderer. She needed to think about who else might have a motive for the killings.

"Can I go see her at the hospital? Is she well enough to have visitors?"

A sweet thought, but probably not useful yet to a woman who was unconscious. "Call them later and ask. That's what I'm going to do. They're being very protective of her there," Lydia told him, omitting the details of the armed guard. "Will you keep looking after her cat and bringing in her mail? If you can't, let me know and I'll do it."

"I can do it," Stuart assured her. "Since the cops requested that I cancel my shoot abroad, I'm kind of at loose ends." Lydia was interested to hear that they wanted Stuart to stay in the country. Once they checked out his alibi, hopefully he'd be able to travel again.

Lydia carried her third cup of coffee into the D'Angelos' office. Her body ached in odd places from her adventure and she had a truly spectacular bruise on her shoulder, but she didn't visibly seem injured. She limped like an old woman, and she vowed to treat herself to that spa treatment as soon as she could stand the thought of someone massaging her body.

The first person Lydia saw in the office was Frankie. He looked like he'd been crying. He was sitting at his desk, staring glumly at the sports section.

"Good morning," she said brightly. He looked at her expressionlessly. His resemblance to his brother, Leo, had never been so pronounced. He had gone from happy-go-lucky to Mr. Gloom and Doom. Lydia instantly felt guilty. She tried to remember what mistakes she'd made recently, but she honestly couldn't recall spending that much time in the office. She buried her head in some paperwork on her desk, hoping to avoid any flying bullets.

Leo practically skipped in fifteen minutes later. As she watched his entrance, astonished, Leo gave her a slow and deliberate wink. She nearly fell out of her chair in shock. The D'Angelo brothers had apparently switched personalities the night before. There was no other reasonable explanation for the phenomenon.

Frankie could not sit still once Leo arrived. He paced around the office until finally walking out without any explanation. He usually hung around, distracting them from their work by reading aloud from the paper, so this behavior also was very unusual.

"What flew up his behind?" Lydia asked.

"He and Heather broke up," Leo said, leaning back with a big grin.

Lydia, forgetting her battered body, leaned forward, fascinated. "Did you find out something?"

Leo nodded. "Oh yeah. Turns out she's really a housewife in Westchester who likes to play around. A friend of mine followed her back to her house after yoga class and found out all about her real life."

"She's married?" Lydia didn't know why she was shocked. Working for two detectives could make you cynical fast about love and marriage. No one in a happy relationship ever asked for a private eye to follow his or her spouse around.

"To an orthopedic surgeon, and she has two kids." Leo looked really proud of himself, like he had discovered the Holy Grail.

Lydia tried to imagine what would motivate someone to risk it all with someone like Frankie. He was nice enough, and perhaps his job as a private eye held a certain allure, but he certainly wasn't God's gift to women. "Poor Frankie."

Leo shrugged and got back to work. He had only cared about releasing his brother from the woman's clutches, not finding out what motivated Heather. He acted like a guy who had never fallen in love.

Lydia sat for a moment at her desk, wondering about all those people who went about their normal lives while hiding something horrible and deceitful from everyone around them. The killer was likely someone she knew, someone who pretended to be her friend, all the while plotting to kill her and her friends. She would never get back to her own normal life, and never again get a good night's sleep, until she found out the killer's identity.

Chapter 31

Every car that backfired made Lydia jump. Every truck that drove just a little too close to the curb made her flinch. She watched people jaywalk recklessly and could not believe that once she had done the same thing. She didn't feel up for riding her bike or taking a subway or bus. There were too many strangers and she would feel too exposed. She decided to call a car service to take her back to the hospital to visit Emily.

Lydia had to use all her wiles to convince the doctors, nurses, and cops at the hospital to let her in to visit Emily. A big skeptical-looking cop on guard duty called in to confirm her story with Romero. He also scrutinized her photo ID as if he was sure it was a fake. Annoying as this was, Lydia was relieved that Emily was in safe hands.

The hospital room was utilitarian and ugly. The walls were painted a soft green, presumably chosen as a soothing shade that had aged to the color of barf. The pink flowered curtains hung limply from metal rods and looked like they had seen better days.

"Emily?" Lydia said softly, and approached the hospital bed.

Emily was lying in the bed with several IVs and machines beeping around her. The machines made Lydia wonder if her condition had taken a turn for the worse. Emily looked up and stared at Lydia with almost no recognition. As Lydia got closer, Emily attempted a smile and winced at the effort. Her face was bruised and battered.

"I didn't recognize you. They won't let me wear my contacts yet." Relieved that Emily was back, Lydia leaned over and gave her a gentle kiss on an uninjured section of her cheek.

"You gave us a big scare," Lydia said, sitting down in the chair next to the bed. She heard the strident cheerfulness in her voice and hoped she didn't sound too fake. "How are you feeling?"

"Like I was tied up in a van for three days," Emily said, wrinkling her nose as she moved her arm. "They told me that you rescued me."

Lydia shrugged modestly. If she hadn't felt somehow responsible that Emily had been kidnapped in the first place, she would certainly have felt prouder of her accomplishment.

Emily looked tired and haunted. The woebegone expression in her eyes tugged at Lydia's heart. She wanted to tell Emily lots of funny stories to distract her, but she didn't think it would work. Emily still looked too traumatized to find anything funny.

Lydia sat with her for a moment, staring at the white hospital sheet. "Did you get a good look at him?"

"Who? The kidnapper?"

"I think he's the one who killed Jenny and Marie," Lydia said. "I figured you got too close to him and that's why he went after you."

Emily shook her head. "I don't know who he is. He was wearing that ski cap when he grabbed me. He threw me in that van and I fought and fought. But he gave me some kind of injection that conked me out. I'm just lucky he hadn't killed me before you found me."

Lydia tried not to think about what would have happened if she hadn't managed to rescue Emily and escape. "Did he talk to you at all? Did his voice sound familiar?"

"He whispered. But I didn't recognize his voice." Emily's fatigue made her sound almost indifferent to the killer's identity. Lydia wondered if she was just tired of having to answer the same questions from the police again and again.

"I didn't recognize him, either. I was too busy running away." Lydia's attempt at a smile failed miserably. "I really hoped you would know who the killer is. . . ."

"Sorry," Emily said.

Lydia decided it was time to throw down the gauntlet. "You don't think it could possibly be Stuart, like the police thought?"

Emily looked at her with wide eyes. Accusing Stuart seemed to have jolted her awake. "Of course not. Why would he do something like that?"

Lydia didn't think he had, but she wanted Emily to tell her more. "To get his stolen tripod back and save his relationship with his client."

Emily closed her eyes briefly. "I'm the one who took it back."

"When?"

"After Marie was dead. She couldn't use it anymore, and I didn't want the police to use the serial number to trace it back to Stuart's client. They had already registered it as a stolen item to collect insurance."

"Why did you want her calendar? Did she put something incriminating in there?" Lydia wasn't going to tell her that she had read over the calendar but hadn't been able to find anything out from it.

Emily looked resigned. "I should have guessed you would find out about that. She told Stuart that if he ever tried to steal anything again, she would go to his client and tell them the serial numbers that she'd seen on his equipment. I assumed she'd written them down in her calendar or something. But I couldn't find it in her apartment."

Lydia thought about how Emily had gone to Marie's apartment under the pretext of helping Marie's family clean up and get ready for the memorial service, but really she had been covering Stuart's tracks. She hated knowing that her friend had done something so deceitful, but she also knew that Emily had suffered emotionally for it. She was too honest not to have. She had also suffered enough for a million transgressions at the hands of a serial killer. Lydia decided it would be best for them all to forget it had ever happened.

"Do you know why Marie left you money in her will?"

Emily shook her head sadly. "She knew I was struggling with my rent and that my family had refused to bail me out. They always wanted me to be a doctor, and they were disappointed when I decided to become a photographer and moved to the city. I felt guilty because I owed them a lot for adopting me. Up until our fight about Stuart, Marie had always been my biggest supporter. I think Marie wanted to make sure that if anything happened to her, I wouldn't give up my dream."

Lydia smiled sadly. Marie had been kind and generous with her friends, even when they had not deserved it. She had tried to keep Stuart on the straight and narrow, and she had given Emily encouragement to keep her pursuing her dream. She wasn't sure what Marie's motivation was exactly concerning Jeanne, but she wanted to believe she'd had good intentions. She hoped that Marie's short time with Jenny had been truly happy, because she had deserved a full lifetime of happiness.

"Is the guard still outside?" Emily asked fretfully.

"Yes, he's there."

"If they don't catch the killer soon, I don't know how I'm going to ever feel safe again."

Lydia wasn't sure she'd feel safe even if they caught the killer. Having one guy behind bars wouldn't make a real dent in the crime rate or change Williamsburg back into a safe haven. It was all about perception, and either hers was now completely screwed up or she was beginning to see the world as it really was.

Chapter 32

When Lydia got back to Georgia's at the end of the day, she searched around inside her almost-empty refrigerator until she located a beer that had rolled over behind some old Chinese food leftovers on the bottom shelf. Lydia didn't bother to look for anything edible. Georgia and she were both order-in kind of gals, and they'd make a call when Georgia came home later. Putting her feet up on an ottoman, Lydia tried to feel at home in a place that wasn't hers. She hadn't realized how much her crummy apartment meant to her until she couldn't go home to it. She missed her clothes, her bed, and even her piles of junk.

She wondered if the only way she'd ever feel safe again would be if she moved. But it was impossible to get a good deal on an apartment these days. She had seen terrible apartments advertised for astronomical sums, and she didn't have that kind of money. She would hate to leave the neighborhood; Williamsburg was where she lived and where all her friends lived. To be driven out of her home by a murderer would be like waving a white flag in defeat. She would have to find a way to be comfortable in her place again, even though it would probably never feel the same.

Her cell phone began tweeting somewhere in the kitchen. She hoped she hadn't put it someplace stupid like the refrigerator. The birds got louder and louder, and the sound was getting on her nerves. She was going to have to change her ring. She got up and went to search for it.

Georgia's kitchen had more kitschy 1950s cooking-related stuff than food. Georgia was strictly a party cook. She liked to do cute hors d'oeuvres and exotic mixed drinks, but she wasn't much for substantial meals.

Lydia finally found her phone behind a set of little Dutch boy and girl salt and pepper shakers. She had no idea why she had stuck it there.

Romero was calling. Her heart started beating fast. Was Emily okay? Was Georgia? She answered quickly.

He didn't waste any time. "I just wanted you to know that it's all over."

Lydia staggered back to the couch and tried to steady her breathing. She was safe. They had captured the killer. "Who is it?"

"Stuart. We arrested him an hour ago for the murders of Marie, Jenny, and Carrie Lamott."

"Stuart? He did this?" She tried to picture Stuart killing Marie and Jenny and destroying her apartment. She had her suspicions when she had found out about the tripod and his fight with Marie, but he still had seemed like such a gentle soul.

"We did a little digging into his past. His half sister was named

Carrie Lamott. Carrie was a runaway, and she was murdered in 1981."

Lydia couldn't stop herself from gasping. "I based the photograph of Marie on her." She had known that Stuart had a sister who died, but she didn't know she had been murdered. She had never learned his sister's name, either. Lydia tried to remember if she had spoken to Stuart about the case or shown him the photograph of Marie, but she couldn't recall. "Why would he kill someone like his sister? He must have been just a kid."

"He's forty-five, so he was eighteen in 1981. We're trying to prove right now that he did both the original murder and the copycat one. He was in New York when his sister was murdered."

Lydia shook her head, trying to clear the cobwebs from her thoughts. "But what about the others? Why would he kill the other models?"

Romero sighed. "Why does anyone kill? The serial killer's mind usually only makes sense to him. He probably hates all women, and killed the other victims because he associated them with his sister. His mind isn't rational."

"Thank you for telling me. I'll let Georgia know that she's safe again." Lydia closed the phone and sat on the couch limply. She remembered her beer, grabbed it, and took a big swig. She was having trouble processing it all. The man she knew was so different from the monster Romero was telling her he was. She hated being alone with her thoughts, so she reached over and grabbed the remote for the TV. Georgia loved HBO, so she had sprung for cable a long time ago. Lydia began blindly to go through the channels. The cartoons seemed too cheerful, the sports too trivial, and the cop shows too violent. Luckily, Georgia breezed in just as Lydia was about to go through all the TV channels for a second time, and she gratefully switched it off.

"They arrested Stuart today."

Georgia gasped. "Why?"

Lydia explained Romero's reasoning. Georgia made appropriate sounds of horror and disgust as she told the story. "I can't believe I could be so wrong about someone."

"Me, either." She remembered how she had encouraged Emily to ask Stuart out, and felt guilty.

"So it's over?"

Lydia nodded, thinking about Marie and Jenny, and about young Carrie Lamott. They all had people who missed them when they were gone. He was a despicable monster if he had killed them all. But there was a big *if* in her mind. Something didn't feel right.

Georgia took off her shoes and rubbed her feet. She had painted her toenails with sparkly blue nail polish. "You don't look convinced."

"I just can't believe . . ."

"That it was someone you know?"

"Yes, and I felt bad for suspecting Stuart. But I can't help thinking that there's something that doesn't add up."

Georgia shook her head and stood. "I feel like pizza tonight. How about you?"

Lydia shrugged. She wouldn't have minded something lighter, but she was trying to be an accommodating guest. Georgia was very sweet to put up with her, especially at such short notice. They were both people who liked their privacy, and they'd probably stayed friends so long because they had never been roommates.

"Black olives and mushrooms from Mama's, right?"

"Sure." She had just enough to cover it. Paying for dinner was the least she could do for taking over Georgia's place as a safe house. She supposed she could go home now, but she felt unsettled. It was better to be with a friend when she felt this way.

Georgia whipped open the veggie drawer in the fridge to reveal her secret stash of beer and cracked one open. "I just dropped in to see Emily. She said you were just there."

"Yeah," Lydia said sadly. "I wish I could do more."

"What are you talking about? You're like some kind of superhero or something. You get tossed in the van and you manage to escape with Emily. I was a little embarrassed to have to hear the whole story from Emily, who only had it secondhand because she was unconscious." Georgia chided her gently.

Lydia grimaced. She'd felt so exhausted after the kidnapping, and mad at herself for getting grabbed in the first place, that she hadn't given Georgia many of the details. "I was scared to death."

"Who says superheroes aren't scared? Martina should give you an *A* in the class and get it over with." Georgia took a big swig of beer.

Lydia had kept so many of the sordid details of the murders from Georgia, but she didn't feel obliged to do so any longer. Perhaps Georgia would have some good ideas when she was presented with all the evidence. She told her about the missing prints, the photo messages she'd received, and how the murderer had posed each of the victims as they had appeared in her photographs. "The murderer has to be someone I know. No one unfamiliar with my work, and someone who didn't know my models, could have done it."

Georgia turned pale when she heard the details. Once the shock wore off, she would probably be angry that she'd been kept in the dark. Lydia quickly gave her all the facts she knew about the murders. Georgia was so familiar with the photographs that she was able to fill in a lot of the details herself.

"Stuart was trying to make it look like you'd killed them?" Georgia said in disbelief. "He must be totally out to get you."

Lydia finally remembered what was bothering her. Stuart was a big muscular guy. The kidnapper/killer who'd grabbed her and put her in his van was strong, but he wasn't big. He was a small skinny guy. She thought she had described him well enough for the cops, but maybe she hadn't been specific enough. Stuart had also told her he had an alibi for that night. If he wasn't lying, either Stuart had an accomplice or he wasn't the killer.

"If it wasn't Stuart, then who was it? The murderer had to know where I took each photograph in order to place the bodies there. I always thought Marie must have known him." Lydia picked at the label on her beer. It was painful for her to go over the details of the murders.

"Why Marie and not Jenny or Emily?"

"First of all, I didn't know Jenny that well, so she didn't know all that information. And second of all, Marie was first, so she seems the most important. But I suppose there has to be some kind of connection linking everyone to me."

"What about Emily? She helped out on a lot of shoots. Maybe she told someone about it, not knowing they would use it against her."

"I thought about Emily. But I can't really see her talking about my pictures. Posing was really uncomfortable for her, and I think she was glad to forget about it."

Lydia suddenly remembered the birthday party pictures of Marie's that she'd put in her suitcase. Marie had invited everyone she knew to the parties, so it was possible that the murderer could be in one of the pictures. Georgia knew way more people than she did, so maybe she'd recognize more of the guests. Lydia bent down next to the couch and rummaged through her suitcase. The photo packet was under a silky nightgown from the fifties that Lydia had been happy to find intact.

Lydia held up the packet. "Remember Marie's birthday party last year?"

"Absolutely. We both looked h-o-t, I don't mind saying." Georgia reached over and clinked her beer bottle against Lydia's.

"I loved Marie's parties. They were never quite what you expected."

Lydia opened the photo sleeve and pulled out the photos. She passed over the group shot of Georgia, Emily, herself, and Marie without a word. She loved the picture, but it was too painful to look at right now, with Marie dead and Emily in the hospital. She systematically went through the stack to see if she might have missed some vital clue before passing the photos on to Georgia. She hadn't looked at the pictures in a while, so it felt like she was seeing them for the first time. In one of the pictures, Pip hovered in the back, next to the bar. He didn't have a beard in the photo, and it took a moment for her to recognize him.

Georgia peered at the photo and then looked up, horrified. "It's the stalker!"

"The what?" Lydia asked, confused.

"It's Phillip, the guy who was stalking me. I didn't really know him then. He became a big problem later. Remember? He started by going to every performance the band gave and staring at me."

Lydia looked at her blankly. She had known that the stalking incident had made Georgia quit performing with the band and join the theater group, but Georgia had not shared so many of the details before. She had a tough motorcycle gang boyfriend named

Walter at the time and Georgia slept at his house when she was scared. Lydia had been ready to help, but she hadn't been needed at the time.

"I remember the stalker, but I guess I never caught his name. Pip is in my art-critique group, and no one ever said he was the same guy. He even spoke at Marie's memorial service."

"I know. It was awful. It was hard for me to get through the last song. I had to rush home afterward."

"I'm so sorry. Emily would never have invited him to speak if she'd known." Lydia felt horrible that she hadn't known to step in and protect Georgia from Pip.

"I tried to keep everything quiet. I guess I didn't want people to know how scared I was." Georgia got up and walked around the room restlessly. "It was so awful. He started calling my phone all the time and leaving messages. I had to change my number. And then he broke into my apartment and stole personal stuff."

Lydia was getting a chill at the back of her neck. "What kind of stuff?"

"He took notes and photos off my fridge. He went through my mail. He listened to my answering machine. It was really disturbing." Georgia shuddered as she looked around the apartment. "I couldn't sleep at my home for weeks. I got a restraining order, but everyone knows those things are a joke."

Somewhere in what Georgia had said there seemed to be an important clue. But, as always, Lydia was drawn to the photos first.

"What kind of pictures did he steal?"

"I think there were some childhood pictures of me, and then some of the Polaroids I took on your shoots."

Lydia felt that prickly feeling on her neck again. This time, it felt like a herd of spiders creeping up her spine. "Polaroids?"

"I always took a Polaroid of the model or had the assistant take a Polaroid if I was the subject. I needed to be sure that the makeup and clothes were the same if we had to change positions and stuff. It was kind of funny to see them in color, since you always worked in black and white. And then I would write the date and the location on the back."

Lydia had never realized that color was such an important clue. When everyone else had looked at her photographs, they'd seen the murders in black and white. But the killer had somehow known what color the clothing was for the models and had dressed them accordingly. Lydia rubbed her arms. Phillip Ensler was the killer they had been looking for. Here was the evidence they had been searching for all along. He had found the locations of each of Lydia's photographs printed neatly on the back of Georgia's Polaroids. He'd had no problem setting his crimes in exactly the same spots as Lydia had used. They had to find Pip and stop him.

"How did Marie meet Pip?"

"I think they were roommates at some point. They stayed in touch, despite what happened to me. Marie thought I had exaggerated the whole thing. We had a big fight about it, and I never felt comfortable with her afterward. I also thought she would keep inviting Phillip to her parties, so I didn't go anymore." Lydia knew that Georgia and Marie had argued, but she hadn't known the cause. She would have thought Marie would have been more sympathetic to Georgia. Perhaps her blind trust in Pip had cost Marie her life.

"I was in his loft, and he had a big room that was locked. I didn't think anything of it at the time, but now I wonder what was inside." Lydia shuddered.

"He was a painter, but he did contracting work on the side—carpentry and that kind of thing. He built some cabinets for Marie in her apartment. But I can't imagine how she could have stood to have him in the house."

Lydia remembered the hammer she'd picked up to defend herself with in the back of the red van. Phillip must have been the one who'd kidnapped her and Emily. But his motivation was still unclear to her. He had worked so hard to set everything up so symbolically, but the meaning was lost on Lydia. Did he hate all women and had just chosen her friends as his victims?

"He's got to be the murderer. There's too much evidence against him. But I don't get why he would want to murder Marie. It sounds like she was one of his biggest fans."

Georgia hugged herself tightly and looked frightened. "I kept telling everyone he was dangerous, but they just thought I was exaggerating. Everyone in the band told me he was just a fan in love with me. But I knew he was dangerous. I wish Marie had listened to me."

His first target had not been Marie, but Georgia. Georgia was the key. He could very well try to make Georgia his next victim. He also had tried to kidnap Lydia, and he might believe that she could identify him. He knew where Georgia lived, and he knew that Lydia and Georgia were friends, so he would know exactly where to find them. Lydia suddenly realized that they were both in serious danger. Pip had to know they were smart enough to put all the pieces together.

"I'm going to call Romero," she told Georgia. "He'll know what to do."

Georgia looked relieved. "I want to call Emily and make sure she's okay."

Lydia ducked into Georgia's kitchen to get a little privacy. She dialed Romero's number with shaking hands. She got his voice mail.

"Detective Romero? It's Lydia. Listen—I think I know who killed Marie and Jenny. I don't think it's Stuart. The killer has to be Phillip Ensler. He stalked Georgia last year and she got a restraining order. He knows where Georgia lives, so it's only a matter of time before he comes looking for us. Please call me back as soon as you get this message." She felt slightly better now that she'd done something, but she still felt helpless. She felt like one of those cartoon characters that was strapped to a ticking time bomb.

The only other number she had for Romero was the one at the precinct. The police officer working the phones said she would convey Lydia's message to Romero. Lydia wondered if she should ask the woman to send a police officer to the apartment, but she didn't think the officer would just because she asked for it. Romero would know how to help them.

She went back to the living room and sat down next to Georgia on the couch. She couldn't sit still, though. She was a bundle of nerves. She wondered how safe Georgia's apartment was. At least she had decent locks on her door. She took a walk past the windows and was relieved to see the bars. They seemed to be somewhat secure. She remembered that Pip had broken in once before, but then she reminded herself that Georgia had updated her security since then. Lydia realized that the beer had caught up with her and she needed desperately to pee.

The bathroom was just off the living room. Georgia was speaking quietly and urgently into her phone when Lydia walked over to grab her purse. Lydia hoped Emily was doing okay. The best thing they could do was to make sure Pip was behind bars and couldn't hurt anyone again. It was too late for Marie and Jenny, but the rest of them were still alive and fighting back.

After Lydia had emptied her bladder, she hunted around in

Georgia's medicine cabinet for beauty products. A little pampering went a long way in relieving stress. Georgia always got great free samples from the salon. She found some moisturizing face wash and gave her face a scrub. It helped her think more clearly and look a little less bleary. She began to sniff the hand cream samplers to find one with a pleasing scent. If she had one on her hand that stank, it was hard for her to concentrate. She didn't like the lily of the valley stuff, so she dug around for something else.

She heard the doorbell ring. "Thank God," she muttered to herself. Romero had gotten there in record time. She sniffed the Tangerine Surprise and thought it smelled good.

She heard Georgia call out, "Pizza! The five-letter word that gladdens every man, woman, and child's heart." Lydia squirted some hand cream on her palm and began to rub it in. Georgia opened a bunch of locks and then there was silence. She remembered she hadn't given Georgia any money for the pizza. She'd have to pay her back.

"Hey, Georgia Rae, remember me?" she heard a man say. Lydia froze. The pizza man wouldn't know Georgia's name. Something was horribly wrong.

"Yes, Phillip, I remember you."

Pip Ensler had easily breached Georgia's locks and security system and was inside.

Chapter 33

Lydia leaned forward and grasped the bathroom sink to hold herself up. Her hands felt wet and sweaty from the hand cream. She thought she was going to be sick. She suddenly hated the way the Tangerine Surprise smelled. They were stuck in an apartment with the serial killer who was out to get them both. Georgia had let him in without looking through the peephole, and now they were at his mercy.

She took a few deep breaths. She had to think of some way to save them both. Her message for Romero had gone to voice mail. He might be in an interrogation room and wouldn't check his messages for hours. She could call 911, but her cell phone was in the kitchen. She cursed herself for not bringing it with her into the bathroom.

She looked around for a weapon. Her purse was sitting on the floor of the bathroom, where she'd dropped it. She opened it up and pawed through it. She had a hairbrush, a camera, and nail scissors. Nothing great. She didn't have any Life Savers left, either. She looked around the bathroom. Georgia had a toilet plunger with a flamingo head and a plastic toilet brush in a rose-shaped holder. Neither looked very sturdy. Under the sink there was some bleach and other cleaning products. She guessed she could throw them in his face, but she wasn't sure she wanted to get close enough to do that.

She didn't want to leave the bathroom, but she didn't want him to hurt Georgia, either. She stood in the center of the space, paralyzed. She could hear their voices, but not at all clearly. What was he saying? She couldn't hear through the closed door.

Lydia very quietly turned the doorknob. If she opened the door just a crack she hoped she could hear what was going on. It opened outward, so she could only open it slightly without calling attention to herself. She almost gasped out loud when she saw Pip through the crack. He was standing just ten feet away, holding a pizza box and a gun. He must have mugged the pizza man to get their delivery.

"Did you miss me?"

Lydia put her head closer to the opening and caught a glimpse of Georgia Rae's profile for a moment. She had turned so pale that Lydia was afraid for a moment she was going to pass out from fear. Lydia needn't have worried. Georgia was made of sterner stuff. She did what any southern woman does when faced with unequal odds: She used bravado.

"Sure. You pestered me like a greenfly for months. It took some serious bug spray to get you out of my hair." Pip's grip on the gun tightened and the pizza box wobbled. Lydia pressed her hand to her mouth so he wouldn't hear her gasp. She hoped that Georgia would keep him talking and give her a chance to figure out what to do.

"I almost didn't recognize you with that beard."

Pip fingered the dark beard. "I thought you would like it."

Lydia frowned. She hoped Georgia wouldn't say something

foolish and make him angry. He didn't need much provocation to kill, apparently.

Georgia shrugged as if it didn't make a difference to her. "Thanks for bringing up the pizza. You want a beer to go with it?"

Pip looked pleased that the object of his affection was finally behaving the way he wanted her to. "You got a Sam Adams?"

"Sure," she said. "Or I can make you a mixed drink." Even while being held hostage, Georgia remembered to be a good hostess.

Lydia hoped he would say yes. Then possibly Georgia could get her hands on a knife. But she knew Pip was a beer drinker. "Just a beer for me."

They moved into the kitchen and out of Lydia's sight. She thought briefly about dashing to the front door and getting out, but she couldn't leave Georgia alone. Besides, he could see the front door from the kitchen, and she didn't need a bullet in her back. She pressed her ear against the opening but she couldn't hear what they were saying. She hoped he wouldn't try anything funny in the kitchen. Meanwhile, he hadn't thought to look in the bathroom, so she had a few minutes to improvise some kind of weapon.

She looked at the flamingo head again. Maybe if she pried the rubber plunger off of the handle, she could tie the nail scissors with dental floss on top to make a sword of sorts. It was worth a try. She picked up the plunger, trying not to think about where it had been, and began to try to wedge the scissors between the rubber and the stick to get the rubber off. It was really stuck on.

Georgia and Pip came back in the living room. Lydia tried to scrape off the rubber quietly, but it still wouldn't come off. She cursed it for being too well constructed. If Georgia had just bought some cheap toilet plunger, she probably could have had the rubber off in thirty seconds.

"A toast, a toast!" Georgia said.

"To what?" Pip asked, looking mystified.

"To life and to love," she said. Pip clinked his beer bottle with Georgia's and stared at her longingly.

"When I saw you up on the stage for the first time, I thought you were the most beautiful woman I'd ever seen. Why'd you quit the band?"

"The attention was a little too much to take," Georgia said. "I needed a break."

"That band never was up to your talents. When that Brian guy started bothering you and asking you out, I ran him over on his bike. He never saw me coming." Pip chuckled. "I'm just sorry I didn't kill him." Lydia remembered Brian's broken arm. He had said he had been hit by a van. Georgia Rae turned a pale green color, and Lydia's stomach didn't feel much better.

"Your singing inspired me. I started doing these amazing paintings. They were all about you and us. I wanted to show them to you."

Lydia thought of the weird muddy paintings in his loft and grimaced. She hoped Georgia would never see them.

"I tried to get a gallery to show them. I thought that if you came to the gallery and saw my art, you would understand how much I loved you." Pip sounded petulant, like a two-year-old boy deprived of his toy. "When no one would show them, I got angry. They show shit every day in those places, and they can't recognize true art anymore."

"Some of them show good stuff," Georgia said. "Like Lydia's work." Normally, Lydia would have loved for her best friend to defend her, but right now she preferred having Pip not think of her at all. But so far, he was showing remarkably little fear or curiosity about what was behind Georgia's bathroom and bedroom doors. She had to find a way to exploit his overconfidence.

"Lydia's work!" Pip snarled. "You wouldn't pose for me, but you posed for her. I saw you in her pictures, looking dead. I would have made you beautiful, but now it's too late."

Georgia smartly said nothing to this, just took a sip of beer. Lydia abandoned the toilet plunger. The rubber was not going to come off the stick. She went back to her bag, hoping by some miracle to unearth a cell phone or some kind of weapon. She was desperate.

"When Lydia got that show, I knew you were going to be so happy. So I thought of a way to ruin it for you both. The cops would suspect her, of course, and then you would both have to beg me to help you. Only I could help you and stop the killing."

"Why Marie? I thought you were friends?" Lydia remembered Martina's words—you only had one chance with an attacker, so you had to make it count. The element of surprise was everything when dealing with a stronger person. He already knew she was resourceful from their last encounter, but Lydia hoped his defenses were down due to the beer and Georgia's excessive friendliness. Lydia put her hand on her camera again. It was heavy and had a strap. She could try to swing it around and hit him with it. It was the only weapon she could find.

"Marie became annoying. Always bragging about her success with her photographs, her gallery show, and the magazines. And I didn't like that she had posed for Lydia, too. Everyone always helps Lydia, but no one ever wants to help me. They don't know how powerful I am, though."

Lydia put her eye to the crack in the door. Pip was swaggering around the living room, looking agitated and waving his gun around.

"Why Jenny? I mean, Lydia's show was already closed and the police suspected her."

"She got suspicious and confronted me. I guess she remembered something I'd told Marie about you. I had to get rid of her. She was going to ruin everything." Pip giggled a little. "I had a little fun and tortured her first." Lydia had to swallow hard to prevent herself from making a sound.

Georgia managed to keep her cool. "They suspected Stuart. Were you trying to frame him?"

Pip shrugged, as if uninterested in the fate of his friend. "He got off eventually, didn't he?"

Pip seemed to like talking about the killing, and Georgia kept asking questions. "Why did you grab Emily and keep her for so long?"

"I wanted to re-create the photo of the two women killed side by side. I thought that would be a nice touch." Lydia shuddered again when she thought of how close she'd come to being one of his victims. If she hadn't managed to unlock the van door from the inside, she and Emily wouldn't be alive today.

Lydia thought of the lives he'd stolen and how Emily would take a long time to recover from the trauma. She wanted to wipe that smirk right off his face. She hoped she'd get a chance to gouge his eyes out: one eye for Marie and one for Jenny. And then she'd break his kneecaps for Emily. She also hoped that Romero was on the way.

Georgia sighed. "I just can't get comfortable with a gun in the house. Why don't you put down that weapon and we can have some pizza?"

"You just want to take it away from me," he said. "You don't really care about me at all. If you cared, I never would have had to kill people."

Lydia heard the sound of birds tweeting. She held her breath. Her cell phone was ringing. Could it be Romero calling her back? She realized she must have left it in the living room.

Georgia jumped up. "Oh my! I think that's my cell phone. Is it in the sofa? I'm always losing it."

"Don't answer it!" Pip shouted. "Whatever you do, don't answer it!"

"I doubt I'll even find it before it stops ringing," Georgia said as she pulled the cushions off the futon.

Pip waved the gun, alarmed. "I thought I told you not to answer it. What are you doing?"

"I'm just trying to turn it off so we won't be disturbed." Lydia wondered if Georgia was going too far with her act.

Georgia slipped her hand under one of the cushions and emerged triumphantly with Lydia's cell phone. "I knew it was under here somewhere."

"Give it to me!" Pip yelled, grabbing it out of her hand. "This is no joke. I've killed before and I can kill again."

Lydia sincerely hoped Romero hadn't hung up already. If he'd stayed on long enough to hear Pip's announcement, he would know exactly what was going on.

"It's okay. Turn it off if you want," Georgia said, calmly ignoring the gun. "Would you like another drink?"

Pip grabbed the phone and turned it off. Lydia let out the breath she was holding. Would a sudden disconnect make Romero suspicious? She hoped so.

"I can drink a six-pack and not get drunk, so don't even think about trying to get me drunk."

"Ever tried tequila?"

"Yeah, and I've eaten the worm," Pip said with a sneer. "But I'm more in the mood for a striptease."

"You can't be serious."

Pip hit Georgia across the face, and Lydia couldn't contain her gasp. She knew he was violent. He had killed two people. But still the violence felt unexpected. Lydia knew she had to do something before he seriously hurt Georgia, but what?

Georgia lifted her head back up. Her cheek was bright pink. Pip shoved his gun in her face. "Take your clothes off now. I want to see it all. And then we can get to the fun part—taking pictures."

Lydia knew that if she came out of the bathroom right now, Pip would have them both. But if she threw him off his stride, then possibly she could disarm him. The best thing was to make him come to her. She needed something to distract him. She seized upon the one easy solution she had at hand: She flushed the toilet.

She rushed back to the door, afraid to peek out, her camera clutched in her hand.

"What was that? Who's here with you?"

"No one," Georgia protested. "No one is here."

Pip clearly didn't believe Georgia. She heard him come closer and closer. She hoped that Georgia was not in front of him, because she was going to try a risky maneuver. It was her one chance at a surprise attack. She tensed her entire body, ready. She wished she had more muscle mass, but she would have to do her best with what she had. When he was just outside the door, hand closing on the handle, Lydia kicked the door as hard as she could. It flew out, knocking Pip down.

Lydia ran out of the door, adrenaline rushing through her system, swinging her camera over her head by its strap and screaming at the top of her lungs. Pip, cursing and clutching his nose with the hand that held the gun, had landed in a sprawl on top of Georgia. Georgia struggled to get out from under him. As soon as Georgia moved out of the way, Lydia kissed her lovely dependable Nikon good-bye and slammed the camera onto Pip's head.

While Pip lay there stunned from the blow, she didn't let herself stop and stare with wonder. She grabbed the barrel of his gun and twisted it out of his grasp, just like Martina had shown them. It was heavier than the lime green squirt guns.

Panting, she held the gun in a way that looked like she knew what she was doing. Really, she was just imitating old *Charlie's Angels* episodes, keeping her feet wide apart and two fingers on the trigger. "Don't move," she ordered.

Pip writhed on the floor. "You broke my nose!"

"Shut up, or I'll do a lot worse."

Georgia stood to the side with her mouth open. She had been held at gunpoint for fifteen minutes, so it was understandable that she was shell-shocked. Meanwhile, Lydia had had the advantage of hiding and plotting her counterattack. But it was time for Georgia to help out.

"Call the cops!"

Georgia fumbled around on the floor for a cell phone. "I don't know if I can dial. . . ."

Lydia waited while Georgia dialed the police, then stumbled over her address and tried to explain that they had a serial killer held at gunpoint. Pip, meanwhile, was trying to wiggle slowly away toward the door.

"Stay still," Lydia told Pip sternly. She really didn't want to shoot him, and Georgia looked like she could use another task to keep herself from falling apart. "Do you have any rope? We should tie him up."

Pip tried to kick out at Lydia, but she neatly sidestepped his foot. "They were your photos! You're an accessory in this crime! If I go to jail, so will you."

Lydia's fingers tightened on the trigger. She was ordinarily not a violent person, but Pip was pushing it. "I did not kill my friends. And we can talk about copyright protection some other time. Georgia?"

Georgia scurried off to her bedroom to hunt for rope. Pip glared at her. "You wouldn't kill me. . . ."

"Oh yeah? Want to try me?" She hoped she sounded supertough. As was true for most bullies, a little of his own medicine shut him right up.

Georgia emerged from her bedroom a minute later with a handful of scarves in her fist. "Will these work? I thought about using panty hose, but they're probably too stretchy. And they'd get ruined."

Lydia rolled her eyes. This was not the time to worry about things getting ruined. Their lives were at stake. "Okay. Hold the gun while I tie him up."

Georgia took the gun awkwardly. "Whatever you do, don't point it at me."

"This is heavy," Georgia complained.

Lydia approached Pip with the longest scarf, a silk black-and-white polka-dot number, and proceeded to tie his hands. He bent his neck and tried to bite her hand. She moved quickly, staying out of reach to tie her knots. "Behave, or she shoots you in the nuts."

"Let me go!" Pip squealed. Lydia shifted her weight to hold him down more securely. This was one of those rare occurrences where a woman wished she weighed more than usual. Lydia was going to do everything in her power to prevent him from hurting anyone ever again.

Lydia took a long red velvet scarf and began to wrap it around Pip's feet. And when Pip wouldn't stop cursing at them, she gagged him with a pink chiffon scarf. They had just sat back to catch their breath when the cops finally kicked the door in.

Romero was the first one through the door, his gun in his hands.

His eyes looked calm and focused, but his hair looked unusually disheveled. He stopped short when he saw Pip all trussed up in the bright-colored scarves. Wong bumped into his back, and the two uniformed officers bringing up the rear bumped into her. There were now enough guns in the room to start a shop.

"You took too long getting here, Romero," Lydia growled. "We had to get the situation under control on our own."

Romero started to laugh, a big belly laugh that filled the room. The uniformed officers snickered and even Wong cracked a smile. Pip struggled against his colorful silk and velvet bindings but could not get free. Lydia had to admit that he looked ridiculous.

"I was worried we were going to find your bodies in here, but I guess I underestimated you again, McKenzie," Romero said when he'd finally caught his breath.

He cleared his throat and stepped over to stand over Pip. "Phillip Ensler, you are under the arrest for the murders of Marie LaFarge and Jenny Powers. You have the right to remain silent. . . ."

Chapter 34

"Get him, hit him, knock him down!"

Lydia had had some pretty disturbing dreams since she had been kidnapped and then had to go head-to-head with a serial killer. She had managed to fight her way out of every situation, but she still imagined Pip killing Georgia and her. In her dreams, she waited again for the shot from the gun, and woke up breathless and scared again. She was sleeping a lot with the lights on, something she hadn't done since she was a kid. She also had called a locksmith to change the locks and put those dreaded bars on her window. She just wanted to feel safe again.

Right now, she was trying to concentrate on beating up a fake mugger for the final exam in the self-defense class. An ex-cop, and a friend of Martina's, he was covered in protective gear from sports like hockey and football. The women were supposed to be able to hit and kick him as hard as they could without injuring him. It was Lydia's turn, and the entire class was cheering her on.

"Kick him! Hit him! Go, Lydia, go!" They yelled together. A cheerleading squad was certainly helpful in this situation, and she wished they'd been there when Pip had been in Georgia's apartment, or when she was in the back of the van with Emily. Lydia felt she would have done much better in both those situations if she had not felt so alone and scared.

When Lydia had returned to class after Pip's arrest, Martina had gone out of her way to congratulate her on her escape. "You did really good. I hope you were able to draw on something from the class to help you out."

Lydia had only been able to shrug in reply. She'd felt like a total incompetent. And although she had saved herself, she was still racked with guilt about Marie and Jenny, and Emily's trauma. She wished she could have figured out that Pip was the killer sooner and prevented their deaths.

Martina had handed her a card for a support group for survivors of violence and rape. "Almost everyone needs a chance to talk after having an experience like yours. It might be helpful for you to give them a try." Lydia didn't feel like she could go, so she'd decided to give the card to Emily. Emily, she reasoned, needed it much more than she did.

As the days passed after Pip Ensler was hauled away to jail, Lydia wondered why she didn't feel safer and more empowered. She felt scared of her own shadow, convinced that her escapes had simply been a fluke. She read in the paper that he was a schizophrenic who had stopped taking his medication. He had a history of stalking women, and police in Florida had reopened a case involving an ex-girlfriend who had disappeared down there. He had managed to fly under the radar for a long time, but his mental illness and obsession with Georgia, Lydia, and their friends had finally caught up with him.

One of the few people she probably could have talked to about her survivor's guilt was Romero. He probably kicked himself all the time for missing evidence and failing to stop the murders. She had not heard from him, though. He was busy putting the case together against Pip, and she wouldn't have dreamed of bothering him.

Now, Lydia gave two good kicks to the fake mugger's kneecap, a hit to his neck, and then retired from the field to give someone else a chance. She wished she felt the exultation she'd felt in her first class, but now that she'd actually hurt someone and seen others hurt, it didn't have the same sense of triumph and fun. Beating someone up had become disturbingly real.

Georgia gave her arm a squeeze as she went by, and Lydia managed a small smile in return as she went to collect her coat and bag. She knew Martina was watching her go with concern in her eyes. Maybe she would take Emily to that support group and see what it was about. Perhaps talking about her experiences would make her feel better.

Lydia took a week off from work. She told the D'Angelos that she had the flu. She didn't want them to know that she had been involved in a murder investigation and had caught the killer. She wanted to avoid their awkward questions and concern.

She hired a service to give her apartment a thorough cleaning, and then set to work sorting through her clothes. She tried not to mourn each destroyed outfit, but it was difficult. She had spent hours shopping and enjoying all her clothes, and now they were ruined. Phillip Ensler had a lot to answer for. Instead of mooning around about each piece, she decided to go shopping. She found a few new things, but her heart wasn't really in it. She made a side trip to the hardware store and picked out some new paint: Etruscan Yellow, Caliente Red, and Mysterious Blue. She'd avoided improving her apartment for years, always thinking she might move. She could see now that she'd never be able to afford another place in New York, and she wasn't planning to move back to Dayton, Ohio, anytime soon, so she figured she might as well make the best of it and actively improve her home. Getting on a ladder and slapping paint on the walls felt good.

She called her parents and told them as much as she could about what had happened. Just as she expected, they were eager to fly to New York immediately to be with her. She convinced them to hold off for a few weeks. She felt like she needed to sort out her troubles on her own and figure out what she was going to do next.

Normally, Lydia would have used her days off to take photographs, but the unfortunate demise of her Nikon after coming in contact with Pip's head made this impossible. The repairman at the camera store shook his head over the damage and told her not to bother trying to fix it. Her heart broke a little. Her Nikon had been her first professional-quality camera and it had been through a lot with her. She had learned on it, and had always taken good care of it. She didn't regret using it to save their lives, but she mourned its passing.

She didn't have enough cash to buy a new camera. She began wondering if she even should. A killer had used her photographs and he had managed to taint her art in a damaging and lasting way. She wasn't sure she should be a photographer anymore. As horrible as it was to think about giving it up, she wasn't sure if she could even still do it.

Emily finally came home from the hospital. Lydia took her dinner and gave her a book of Dilbert cartoons to cheer her up. Stuart was there, and instead of feeling at ease with them both, Lydia felt that she was intruding. Neither one of them appeared to have forgiven her for suspecting Stuart of murder and bringing up the death of his half sister, Carrie Lamott, again. Her death had ripped his family apart, and it was painful for them to have their loss reported in the media again.

Lydia wondered if Emily and Stuart also felt guilty because Pip had been their friend and they had not suspected how crazy he was. Lydia didn't know for certain. She just wished they could all move on and be comfortable with one another again. She didn't need anyone's gratitude for catching Pip. She had just been trying to defend herself, and she had been luckier than Marie and Jenny.

She took Diana Randolph to coffee one morning, but they didn't talk about the photographs or the murders. They talked instead about the changing neighborhood. Diana's stepchildren wanted her to move into an assisted-living facility, but she relished her independence. Lydia promised to stop in every once in a while to make sure she had everything she needed. Diana's hopefulness despite the darkness helped raise Lydia's own spirits, and she decided she was ready to return to work at the D'Angelos'.

When she strolled into the office, Leo was sitting at his desk, going through the expense reports. He peered at her over his reading glasses. "It's nice of you to join us today, Lydia." Doing expense reports always made Leo grumpy, so Lydia just ignored him.

She went over to her desk and surveyed the mess they'd managed to make while she was gone. There were piles of junk mail dumped in her in-box. There was a pizza box on the floor, and a coffee stain on her desk. She rolled up her sleeves and got to work.

She scrubbed at the stains. She hauled bags of stinking trash out of the office. She felt more like a housemaid than an administrative assistant. It felt good to do some mindless grunt work just the same, but seeing Leo drop a dirty coffee cup into the sink was the last straw. "Don't you guys know how to clean up after yourselves?"

Mama D'Angelo tut-tutted from the doorway. "They don't, Lydia, and I'm afraid it's all my fault."

"That's not fair, Mama," Leo said in a hurt voice.

Mama shook her head. "They still drop off their laundry at my house, even at their age. Disgraceful. But I encourage them because I want my boys to come over. I like doing things for them."

Mama pinched Leo's cheek. "You brought me something, Mama?"

"No, this is for Lydia." Mama carried over a fragrant bag of pastries and a large cappuccino and set it on Lydia's desk.

"For me?" Lydia said, touched. Mama watched her carefully, as if she knew what Lydia had been through in the past week. Mama always seemed to know everything, and Lydia had no idea how she found it all out. Lydia turned her full attention to the treats so she wouldn't have to meet Mama's perceptive eyes.

"You look too tired. They said you had the flu. Make sure you go home early and rest up."

"Do I come in and send your employees at the restaurant home early?" Leo complained halfheartedly.

Mama D'Angelo ignored her elder son. "Don't let these slave drivers work you too hard, honey." Mama walked out, leaving a familiar cloud of Chanel No. 5 and garlic in her wake. Lydia was beginning to find the scent combination endearing.

Frankie came in a couple of hours later, looking tired. Lydia wondered if maybe he really did have the flu. He stopped abruptly inside the door and looked surprised to see Lydia at her desk. Maybe he'd suspected that she'd quit. He put his newspaper carefully down on his own desk, picked up some paperwork, and took it over to Lydia.

“These are from the Santana case,” he told her. “I need you to type up my notes for Monday.”

“Okay,” she said, and put the papers down on top of her in-box. He continued to stand in front of her desk, shifting from one foot to the other. He looked like a little boy who was afraid he was in big trouble. “Did you have something else for me?”

“No. I was just glad to hear that your friend’s murderer was caught. We worry about you walking around on your own.”

“Thanks.” She was glad the cops had kept her involvement out of the papers. She was happy to give the NYPD all the credit on the case. She did not want to tangle with a murderer ever again.

Frankie nodded and smiled at her.

Lydia took a deep breath. “I was thinking it was about time to get a Web site.”

Frankie wrinkled his nose. “What for?”

“To attract clients, of course,” she said. “And I have a form here for putting an ad in the Yellow Pages.”

Frankie had begun to back away from her desk. They clearly saw advertising their services as somehow vulgar, but like those minor royals who’d had to rent out their castles to tourists, the D’Angelos were going to have to adapt to survive. She certainly couldn’t keep working there if they ran out of money and clients.

She decided to wait before springing a few of her other marketing ideas on them. Besides, she had to go change and get ready for opening night of *Stop the Violence.*

The stage lights went down as the last rousing chorus was sung. There was a momentary silence as the audience tried to take in the totality of what they’d seen. *Stop the Violence* was a singing, dancing extravaganza, but it also had a sobering message. The theater erupted into rapturous applause. The lights came up, and all those killed in the course of the play rose up and came back to life in the miracle of the theater. All of them had lost their bumps, bruises, and scars and became whole again. The audience applauded even louder.

Lydia was conscious of Detective Romero occupying the armrest between their two chairs. She tried to ignore him, but the warmth where their bodies touched distracted her. She felt odd seeing him again. They had bonded in a strange way through the adrenaline of fear and the capture of a criminal. Now he was like a stranger.

Each member of the ensemble came forward to take a bow. Lydia whistled and cheered loudest when Georgia stepped up with a grin. The message of the play had been a little didactic, but it was important nonetheless. She thought they could have given Georgia more songs to sing, considering how talented she was, and how often they'd insisted she attend rehearsals. Georgia spotted Lydia in the audience and threw her a kiss as the actors walked off the stage.

The cheers continued, and the group came out onstage again to take another bow. Then Georgia stepped out in front and raised her hands for quiet. It took a few moments for the crowd to calm down, but at last they did.

"Thank you so much for your warm response to our performance tonight. This play was written to reach beyond this room and hopefully affect public policy and the world with our message of peace and nonviolence." Georgia sounded cool and collected, but Lydia could see the shadows under her eyes. The experience with Phillip had left her shaken. The last time, Georgia had been able to conquer her fears by installing all the locks and bars on her apartment. Now, Lydia wasn't sure what Georgia could do to make herself feel safe again.

"In that spirit, members of the community collected money during rehearsals to be given to anyone who could catch and stop a killer in our neighborhood, a killer who had taken the lives of two of our friends, Marie LaFarge and Jenny Powers. Tonight we are happy to acknowledge Detective Daniel Romero and Lydia McKenzie. Through their hard work, persistence, and bravery, a killer was brought to justice, and we hope the spirits of our friends may now safely rest.

"Although Detective Romero is unable to accept a cash reward for his work, he will accept the award on behalf of the Police Athletic League." Georgia beckoned with her hand to Lydia and Romero.

Lydia reluctantly rose and walked up to the stage, followed by Romero. This was the part of the evening she had been dreading. As a photographer, she was content to stay behind the scenes. She'd done her best with her appearance, though. On her latest shopping spree, she had found a 1970s polyester evening dress covered with a rainbow of crazy paisley patterns. She'd dug up a pair of gorgeous gold sandals that looked like something a rich gladiator would wear, and they suited the dress perfectly. Her hair was back to auburn, and she'd piled it on top of her head in an Audrey Hepburn–like hairstyle. Overall, she was pleased with the effect, but she was still embarrassed by the attention.

Georgia gave Lydia and Romero each a hug. Up close, her makeup looked heavy and smeared. It was hot up under the lights, and Lydia felt her own makeup start to melt.

"The Stop the Violence Theater Group is proud to present each of you with a check for a thousand dollars for your efforts to bring down the Williamsburg killer. We all salute you for your effort and applaud you for your success." Lydia tried not to let her jaw fall open. She had not expected such a large check.

The audience clapped and whistled. Georgia handed each of them a heavy cream envelope. Romero took Lydia's hand and together they took an awkward bow together. Lydia felt unworthy of their applause. A real hero would have prevented the murders from happening altogether. She still found it hard not to feel some culpability for the crimes, since her photographs had been a trigger for the killer. If she had been paying better attention when Georgia'd had problems with her stalker, she might even have prevented the deaths of her friends.

Looking out into the sea of faces, Lydia wondered how many of them had known Marie or Jenny or Pip. Pip had stalked Georgia, kidnapped and traumatized Emily, robbed and kidnapped Lydia, injured Brian and Jacques, and set up Stuart as a suspect. He had also frightened everyone in their neighborhood with his killing spree. She wished the audience could all somehow reach out to the ones they had lost to tell them how important they were and how much they were missed.

Clutching her envelope, Lydia exited the stage, with Romero following close behind. Many of the cast members she had met in the self-defense class surrounded them backstage to congratulate and thank them both. Romero and Lydia shook a few hands and together made their way out of the theater.

"So what are you going to do with your winnings, McKenzie? Want to take a trip to Atlantic City together and do some gambling?" Romero grinned at her. He looked boyish and attractive when he smiled, and she felt a little jolt in her body, as if it were waking up from a long sleep.

Lydia pretended to consider his offer for a moment, even though she knew it was a joke. "Sorry, but I think my bosses have decided that I've taken quite enough time off from work."

Romero twisted his mouth in an exaggerated frown. "You've got to live a little, you know."

"I know," Lydia said softly. She took a deep breath. She suddenly knew what she would do with her money. "I'm going to buy a new camera."

As soon as the words left her lips, she could see the camera she would get, new and gleaming, with an expensive lens and the kind of bells and whistles she never would have been able to afford before.

"Sounds too practical. Haven't you ever tried gambling?"

She smiled. She was a photographer. It was pointless to pretend otherwise. She felt like a weight had been lifted from her shoulders. "Can't say that I have. Unless you count buying a lottery ticket."

Lydia looked at Romero for a moment, wondering sadly if she would ever see him again. During the search for the killer, their lives had intertwined time and time again. But without a common cause, she wasn't sure they'd ever run into each other.

"I was wondering something. Why did you never write down anything I told you in your notebook? You were always scribbling away when you interviewed other people."

"Why do you think?"

"I guess I thought that you didn't think it was important enough."

"Nah. I never needed to write anything down, because I always remembered what you said."

Lydia waited for a moment, trying to figure out if there was a compliment in there somewhere or if she should get miffed at him. Before she could decide, Romero took a small newspaper out of his pocket.

"I saw this the other day, and I wasn't sure if you had a copy." He handed the paper over to her and she accepted it, confused.

"Let me know if you change your mind about Atlantic City. You've got my number." With a jaunty wave, Romero took off, tucking his envelope in his pocket.

Lydia opened up the newspaper, mystified. Inside was a review of her show by a writer at the local paper. He called her "a mysteriously disquieting new find" and predicted she would be going places. The paper had a readership of about one thousand, and no one in the art world read it, but it made her feel better than she had in weeks. As soon as she got that new camera, she was going to get back to work again.